I0577394

i

**Published by Harbor & Stone Press**

Commerce City, Colorado

Harbor & Stone Press is a boutique publishing house for indie authors seeking a fair, reliable, and supportive partner through every step of the publishing process.

www.harborandstonepress.com

@HarborAndStonePress

harborandstonepress@gmail.com

# ROOTED IN SILENCE

## Some Roots Grow Deeper in the Dark

*To my husband Ryan, who inspired this book by being nothing like the characters inside it.*

"Hell Is Other People"

Jean-Paul Sartre

# ROOTED IN SILENCE

Some Roots Grow Deeper in the Dark

## A. M. Walker
Harbor & Stone Press

# Table of Contents

# Author's Note

To My Readers,

While the events and characters in Rooted in Silence are fictional, the psychological territory they explore is one that is often familiar.

Perfect for fans of *The Silent Patient*, *Gone Girl*, or *Breaking Bad*, these stories captivate us because they examine how seemingly ordinary people rationalize psychopathic choices—and how quickly moral lines can blur when someone believes they're protecting what matters most.

Like those narratives, this novel asks uncomfortable questions: What happens when someone's need for control becomes consuming? How do we justify the unjustifiable to ourselves? And what does it look like when the person everyone trusts is the one they should fear most?

The characters in this story aren't drawn from real people, but their psychological complexity reflects something true about human nature—our ability to reframe destruction as protection and the frightening ease with which someone can smile while planning something terrible.

If you've ever been drawn to stories about the darkness hiding behind perfect facades, this book examines that territory through the lens of domestic life, where the most dangerous betrayals often come from those closest to us.

    — A. M. Walker

# Chapter 1:

## Cobwebs

The crawlspace was just as musty and cramped as I imagined, but today I needed a place that could hide secrets. Cobwebs clung to my arms like damp threads as I crawled through the space. An old dryer manual lay there, warped at the edges. We hadn't owned that dryer in two years. The cover was yellowed, curling at the corners.

I'd managed to avoid crawlspaces for as long as I could remember—ever since I was twelve and crawled in my family crawlspace on a dare, only to swear I saw a pale shape shift in the shadows.

But that was when fear ruled me; now it was time to rule fear.

Something crunched beneath my knee. I didn't look down.

Instead, I ducked lower, my head grazing the beams, and made my way toward a Tupperware labeled *EMILY'S COLLEGE JERSEYS* that I kept alongside Remmy's matching one—each Tupperware neatly marked.

This one was different, a hidden capsule Remmy would have no reason to open.

It would serve as the perfect hiding place for my notebook. I ran my fingers over the ivory paper, the pages still scarred where my pen pressed too hard. Now my handwriting looked foreign to me in places, as if I'd been moving too fast to remember I was the one manipulating the pen. Every entry began as curiosity and ended as confession—I couldn't stop cataloging what I learned, as if writing the danger down made it safer, less lonely.

I ached to keep it near, but I felt suspicion around me growing like an unmoving heat clinging to my skin. Even the air down here tasted stale, as if it resented what I was hiding.

The linen-bound reference I'd created contained details on dozens of toxic plant varieties, a set of pressed Foxglove petals glued to the inside cover.

The morning Ms. Volkova passed the Foxglove to me over the fence, I examined the bloom. Each stem contained its full roots, the roots dangling from the dirt like claws.

This bundle contained flowers with nine petals, white with edges bruised raspberry pink. The bloom looked as if it had bled once and healed poorly.

I couldn't explain how I knew, only that the flower carried a power beneath its bashful roots—something far beyond beauty. I'd seen them scattered across

Hermosa Beach, but the fragment she'd pressed into my hand felt weighted, deliberate.

"It's beautiful," I said, my gaze fixed on the flower with edges splashed like blood.

"Most of the time," she whispered, "the most beautiful things are also the most dangerous."

She handed me a bundle as if I'd requested a cup of sugar across the fence.

I held it lightly, unsure whether to feel flattered or afraid. Maybe both—because both required a level of trust I wasn't used to.

I didn't ask what it was. She didn't explain either. The kind of understanding we shared didn't need naming. And without looking back, she walked toward her porch.

It took me a moment to register the weight of what had just passed between us. She'd handed me a weapon disguised as a gift, casual as breath. As if she'd pressed my finger to the trigger and whispered for me to pull. Adrenaline surged—sharp, electric, blinding. I didn't know if it was fear or fascination.

Maybe this was what control felt like—knowing danger and touching it anyway. I began to familiarize myself with that kind of feeling.

A scrape against the wall jolted me back to the humid crawlspace where my fingertips circled the fragile petals embossed on the book's skin.

I entered a new variety—*Nerium oleander*—or oleander as most would know it. I'd first heard of it during a virtual workshop from the community center, *Becoming Your Garden*.

I logged each fact I'd gathered meticulously, my handwriting racing with every line:

*Oleander: glossy leaves slick with sap, flowers that smell faintly of almonds. Even one leaf could still a heartbeat. It thrived in heat, like it needed an audience.*

The plant could adorn a sunny veranda or appear as an innocent bouquet at a wedding—its danger disguised beneath perfume and color.

I couldn't name what drew me to log it—it didn't serve any real purpose. The words lived only inside my notebook. But I was drawn to the knowledge, the background, even the folklore, soaking every detail like a sponge.

Maybe I just wanted to see what could live in both beauty and danger.

Most people's crawlspaces hid dust and junk. Mine hid proof I wasn't like them—proof I wasn't destined for an ordinary life.

I climbed down, whacking cobwebs and dust bunnies like a bird plucking its own feathers. Control began in the crawlspace and followed me upstairs.

A quick glance at my watch. The little hand struck seven. Remmy would be home from his shift at the hospital any moment.

Clean counters meant safety. If everything sparkled, nothing bad could reach him.

If I wanted to stay in control, I had to maintain my image. Order was oxygen.

Every polish and wipe was a prayer disguised as habit. Order was the only thing I could build that wouldn't collapse under me. A single smear, a spoon with hardened gunk—one fatal flaw and the whole illusion could crack. I wiped an already clean counter.

The candle's wick had just ignited when I caught the soft whine of brakes easing to a stop outside. By the time the door opened and Remmy entered the kitchen with a fresh bouquet from the corner shop in hand, I was humming "Marry Me" to the radio—the dial set to eighteen, Remmy's preferred volume—while sprinkling rosemary on a skillet.

I hated the song, but harmony mattered more than preference.

The bouquet he held was harmless—petals dyed and bound with rubber and plastic.

Pathetic, corner-shop roses with no teeth. Ordinary flowers for ordinary people. That would never be me, no matter how much he wanted that.

Anyone watching would have seen domestic contentment. They'd have missed the rehearsal underneath.

"You know, Em, you don't have to scrub the place like there's a magazine shoot every night," Remmy said when he reentered the kitchen. He kissed my cheek but didn't drop it. "Sometimes it's okay if the counter just looks... lived in."

The sauce simmered like my thoughts, thick with herbs. I stirred it twice—a ritual of control—the wooden spoon tapping in rhythm with my thoughts. The granite counter gleamed, reflecting my face like a mirror—except for one dull spot I couldn't polish away.

I scrubbed until it vanished, but the spot stayed in my mind long after.

# Chapter 2:

## Emily and Remy

The wind pressed against my coat, curling strands of hair into my face, but I didn't tuck them back. It was better to let the world think small irritations never touched me.

I'd heard it all before, about how weddings were stressful. The same people often missed the importance of preparation. If you prepared for the worst, nothing could ambush you again. Fear was just poor planning.

I had a date with invoices, a nice break from logistics and calls with overpriced vendors. Numbers are predictable. People and their egos are not.

As I walked back through the breezy suburbs, I crossed 72nd Street and noticed that the coffee shop near City Hall had changed its chalkboard. It read: *Congratulations, Emily & Remy!* Two stick figures held hands beneath a poorly-drawn archway. They even featured my regular: butterscotch cold brew with extra soft foam. The barista stood by the sign, handing an older man a frothy latte. Her smile was bright, her lipstick cherry red.

Everything in the scene was perfect—even the misspelling in Remmy's name. They'd missed an *m*, but that hardly mattered. What mattered was that my name wasn't ordinary anymore, scribbled in chalk like everyone else's. Soon it would be carved into the air, a name meant to linger in whispers.

Besides, people got things wrong all the time.

To them, I was just another fiancé planning a wedding. Forgettable, interchangeable. They didn't realize they'd be remembering me for something else entirely.

I nearly skipped home, all the way up the footsteps. I hummed to the fiddle of my keys unlocking the door.

I couldn't ignore the small power in seeing my name spelled correctly beside his spelled *incorrectly.*

A clank met my keys when I dropped them into the wicker tray on the entry table. The citrus-and-sage diffuser by the kitchen sink had faded, but a faint scent lingered in the air—clean and slightly sharp, like the calm after a deep scrubbing. I liked that kind of sharpness; it reminded me of starting over.

Of closing a door, scrubbing a counter, lighting a match.

I straightened a picture frame on my way to the kitchen. Order steadied my pulse faster than breathing ever could.

The sulfur of a match always made my feet hold more weight.

After cracking two windows, I'd ignited the candle Remmy's mom had bought me last Christmas. It was expensive—a three-wick in a heavy jar, label embossed with gold. It smelled like fig and fir and a French flower I couldn't name.

I slipped off my shoes and set the table. Wine glasses. Cloth napkins folded into uneven triangles. I adjusted the linen runner that matched our wedding palette—eggshell and bone.

The risotto went on low. The squash barely splashed when it met the heated skillet. It was the kind of dinner that looked effortless but wasn't. Poison had the same appeal to me.

Dinner was my stage, a place where I could be Rachael Ray or Gordon Ramsay, anyone but Emily Byrd.

Widowhood, too, was a performance. Society adored the tragic wife, the polished survivor draped in loss. If people were watching, they should see grief perfected. If no one was, I should still believe in the part I was playing.

Remmy walked in at 6:22 p.m.

He dropped his hospital bag by the door—no scuffs, no sagging. His white sneakers were still spotless, as if the hospital had never touched him.

"Hey, Mrs. Almost-Black," he said into my hair.

"Hi, Rem."

"You're glowing." He collapsed into the chair next to me, sighing as he sat—more release than exhaustion.

"I know." I held back my smile.

"You look good." His eyes scanned the table. "What's the occasion?"

"No occasion."

There was a reason, of course—practice always needed an audience.

He raised a brow, smiling. "No occasion for a Michelin kitchen?"

I shrugged. "I didn't want the squash to go bad. And we had that wine we opened on Sunday. Didn't want it to turn."

He thought of it as romantic. I thought of it as practice. And practice was how you made something perfect.

He didn't press. He never did. That was part of it— part of him. He had a way of letting things slide that both drew me to him and made me resent him at the same time. Like he'd never burn energy on the small stuff, even if the small stuff was where the truth lived. I lived there, too.

Sometimes I almost loved him for how easily he forgave the world. *Almost.*

I carried over the plates. He asked about my day, though he didn't need to; I'd already put every to-do in our shared calendar, color-coded and synced to his phone.

He'd thanked me for that a few days ago, saying it was amazing how I *made everything feel effortless.* I could never tell if he truly appreciated my organization or just encouraged what made me feel whole.

"Okay, wow," he said, gesturing toward his plate. "You crushed this."

"I know," I said, sipping water. "You like lemon, and the scallops were on sale." They weren't.

He grinned, still chewing. "God, I love you."

Then he left his scallop knife smeared on the linen runner, oblivious to the small wreckage he left behind.

"You even lined up the napkins. Do you do this for me, or for you?" He smiled before I could respond, but his eyes lingered on mine for a beat too long.

It was quiet for a bit, just forks against ceramic and the occasional clink of his glass. That kind of quiet was the closest thing I had to proof that I'd done the day right.

No sighs, no questions, no interruptions—just the low hum of two people orbiting in sync.

I liked it like this. Calm. Functional. Real. No dramatic gestures. Just the quiet comfort of two people who'd gotten good at being around each other.

After a few bites, I pulled out the seating chart and placed it on the table.

"I shifted your cousins to Table 4. The Johnsons are still at 7. I figured fewer potential landmines."

While I re-did the seating chart for the third time, Remmy hunched over his sketchpad, shading in the legs of a table.

He looked so proud, like graphite lines could hold a family together. His table might last a hundred years, but no one would whisper about it the way they would about me.

He skimmed it briefly, nodding. When he looked up at me, his impressionable eyes were full of admiration. "You really think of every detail. Thank God you do, because I'd never keep it all straight." After his lips met the soft skin of my cheek, he leaned across the counter and poured us each a glass of wine.

He tapped the paper, eyes narrowing briefly. "Funny—you moved my cousins twice already. You sure you're not hiding some secret strategy from me?"

His grin softened the remark, but the question lingered just enough to feel almost dangerous.

"So," I said, changing the subject, "did you look at the song list I sent you, for our final dance?"

"For you, my love," Remmy said, pausing mid-chew and holding up a finger to finish his bite, "I'll dance to anything."

"I want the final dance to be private," I explained. "Just us. Lights dimmed. No photos." My smile twitched before I caught it.

He glanced up, curious. "Private?" I could already see the faint image of the final dance in my mind: the crowd fading into darkness, the room shrinking until it was just us, the music pressing against the walls like it was trying to keep a secret.

"Yeah. Like... a movie scene. No one watching. No cameras, no people. Just us."

Suddenly, I felt a throb in my temples, a ringing in my ears. An image forced its way into my mind.

The lights dimmed, guests blurring into the shadows. A waft of champagne and roses teased the hairs in my nostrils.

Across the room, a cup of tea rested, its steam beckoning me.

We moved in slow circles while the song bent the room around us, a secret folding itself inside the noise.

As we danced, I kept my gaze on the tea—just barely out of reach to grab it.

Remmy's gentle laugh snapped me back into the moment, the image fading from my mind.

"We can have a private last dance, of course," he said. "I don't want you to dream too big, something I can't fulfill."

I couldn't find a response that felt light. He winked to cut the tension. "We're not on set, Em."

I smiled because that was the only response that kept the peace. But I held the picture in my head anyway, like a child clutching a forbidden toy.

By the time he disappeared to shower and change into his pajamas, I was rinsing the plates, loading the dishwasher, and wiping the counters—tasks that only felt satisfying when the rest of your life felt clean.

I cleaned in silence. Noise made me sloppy.

When Remmy reemerged in a T-shirt and sweatpants, his hair damp and flat, I was overwhelmed by the smell of cedar and soap. I handed him a kitchen towel for his hair without thinking, and he took it without comment. These rhythms came without effort now.

When we finally settled onto the couch together, Denver flopped between us. Remmy scrolled through

Netflix, stopping on something crime-related and absurd. "This okay?"

He pulled a notebook from the couch arm—sketches of tables and chairs he wanted to build—and ran his fingers over the pages.

"When this wedding is over, I want to start that side project again—the oak table for the garage. You'll roll your eyes, but one day I'll build us a set that lasts a hundred years."

"Sure," I said. "About the show, I mean." And we left it at that, resting the conversation.

Silence had edges. I liked the way it kept people from bleeding into me.

While the host of the show talked about oak, I thought about linens.

The officiant's voice; the lace on my veil.

About how I'd do it.

How I'd do it without a sound.

He laughed once at something on screen, a short bark that echoed off the walls. I felt it vibrate through his chest but didn't look up.

My to-do list was already rearranging itself in my mind. He rubbed my arm gently, fingers grazing without purpose.

I let my body sink further into him, letting the silence carry the weight I didn't want to name. I'd built this whole thing—this pattern, this rhythm, this picture we were showing the world.

The wedding would be the end of this, but it wasn't the end of *me*. It was the peak. The moment everyone would remember. The version of us they'd lock in their heads forever.

They'd see me, forever stained by the unfortunate fate of our wedding day. The look on neighbors' faces when they learned of the news felt warm, like a shot of sharp whiskey.

Every story needs a perfect ending. I was only making sure mine arrived on time.

Making sure they'd consider me in every room.

That's why everything needed to be flawless. And it almost was.

I thought of Ms. Volkova's yard, always perfectly trimmed; no weed ever dared to appear. She knew the secret—that perfection only thrived when something else was cut away.

Remmy reached for the remote and paused the show. "Actually," he said, "I thought of the song for our final dance."

"Yeah?"

He played the opening bars on his phone—an older track, sentimental without being sappy. I didn't cry, but I let my hand slip into his.

We listened in silence—a kiss, a nod of approval, then the familiar flick of the television.

We watched the rest of the show—or at least he did. I closed my eyes for a moment, trying to imagine the dance floor under low lights: the shape of our silhouettes under the weight of that final moment.

Like a fairytale, no one would expect the ending.

No fairytale bride wanted to be ordinary. My ending would be the only one they remembered.

# Chapter 3:

# Wolfsbane

I took Denver out earlier than usual. The air had that thick, pre-rain smell—cool and damp, like something was hanging from the trees. The kind of morning that made you want to wear a sweatsuit, curl up with a book, and call it a day before it even began.

Denver trotted in his raincoat beside me with lazy energy, pausing to sniff the cement or check on his favorite fence post.

The neighborhood was still half-asleep, but a neighbor I've never met waved from across the street. I waved back slowly, deliberately—like someone with nothing to rush toward. Nothing to hide.

My pace matched Denver's, unhurried and aimless. I realized how rarely I walked without the drum of my next step beating in my mind.

We turned the corner by the old church, the one with peeling white trim and a fading red door.

That's when I saw her.

Ms. Volkova was bent at the waist, kneeling in the Church's side garden. A small gardening knife glinted in her gloved hand as she sliced through stems with the confidence of someone who had perfected its swing.

She hadn't heard us yet, and for a second, I considered turning around. But Denver had already spotted her. He pulled ahead, leash taut.

The first time I met Ms. Volkova, she took the spade from my hand without asking.

"You'll kill it," she said—not cruel, just certain. I should've been annoyed, but I found myself watching her hands instead. They were steady, veined like roots under thin skin. From that moment, she never wasted a word, but she always watched. Like she was deciding whether to prune me or let me grow wild.

From then on, we spoke more, though "more" was relative.

But in this moment, I was the one with the sense to observe. The garden she was working on now had no sign of death. A faint smell of damp earth and something sharper—mint?—hung in the air.

Volkova's back was a straight, deliberate line as she worked, her shoulders moving in precise motions. She straightened at the sound of our steps, slow and stiff, wiping her gloves on a folded towel tucked into her waistband.

"You're up early." Her eyes were fixed on mine.

"Couldn't sleep."

"Busy mind?" Her words came with a bite, subtle but unmistakable.

"You could say that." I forced a small smile. "Just taking Denver out for an early walk."

She shifted her eyes to the church grounds. "You know how to keep your men loyal."

She didn't clarify what that meant. Instead, she turned, bending to pick up a small bucket near her knee and pulling out a neatly tied bundle—dried stems with pale lavender blooms, brittle, and color-faded, bound with twine.

"Here," she said, holding it out.

I took it before I thought to question it. The bundle felt delicate, like it would fall apart if I looked at it wrong.

"*Aconitum napellus*," she said with a slight smirk, testing my background in botany.

I merely blinked.

"We call it wolfsbane," she said, brushing a thumb over the stems. "This plot's best harvest."

I turned it in my hands. "Thank you... What's it for?"

Her tone was casual, but her eyes stayed on me. "Historically? For arrows. And in small doses, medicine." A faint hint of amusement tugged at her mouth. "But for us, it's just decorative."

Denver pawed at the sidewalk, impatient.

"Well," I said lightly, "thanks. I've never been gifted poison before." It felt like a compliment dressed as a dare.

Ordinary neighbors traded sugar or lemons. Volkova handed me danger, because she knew I wasn't built for small talk and sameness.

I rolled the stems in my palm, feeling the brittleness give under my fingers.

It wasn't lost on me that she'd chosen something beautiful enough to touch, deadly enough to punish.

She didn't laugh.

I hesitated. "Why grow wolfsbane in a church garden?"

"Why not?" She crouched back to the soil. "You'd be amazed what people admire so long as it's beautiful. Some of the most dangerous plants in the world are blue and violet."

I opened my mouth, then closed it. Something unspoken hovered between us—not heavy, but insistent. The kind of silence that passes between women who know better than to say everything out loud.

"You're getting married soon," she added without looking up.

"In two weeks."

She nodded. "You remind me of someone."

I didn't ask who. I didn't ask why she had never mentioned that before. I just stood there a second too long, bundle in hand.

"Well," I said finally, "we should get going."

She didn't stop me.

Denver and I turned for home, the stems cracking faintly in my fist. A few flakes of dried flower clung to my skin like ash.

That afternoon, I buried the wolfsbane.

I didn't want it in the house. I didn't want it in the garage either—too dangerous. Too traceable. The last thing I needed was Remmy stumbling upon a random bundle of ashy stems.

So I walked out barefoot, coffee in one hand, bundle in the other. I crossed the yard to the farthest corner, where the rosemary bush had spilled over its borders, climbing past the planter like it had somewhere better to be. It smelled sharp and a little wild.

Remmy always said rosemary reminded him of home-cooked meals. To me, it smelled like effort—like people who could afford the time to slow down and get things right. It smelled like intention.

I crouched, peeled the soil back, and tucked the brittle stems beneath the roots. No ceremony. No second thought. Just gone.

But the roots would still be there, threading through the dark, waiting.

The soil clung to my fingertips, damp and cold. For a moment I imagined the brittle stems pulsing back to life underground, roots threading through the rosemary until the whole bush turned poisonous. I buried it deep.

Nature doesn't care who tends the land, who plants the seed; it only cares what can survive. I pressed the earth down harder, flattening any chance of that. As I patted the dirt back into place, I caught my reflection in the kitchen window—blurred by glare and distance, but still there.

I looked composed. Calm. Like a woman tending to her herbs.

Someone thoughtful. Nurturing, even. Someone who might press rosemary into a roast or dry lavender for tea, just for the appearance it accompanies.

But beneath the surface, something buzzed. Not guilt. Not even fear.

Just a low, steady hum. Like standing near a phone, about to ring.

\*\*\*

Throughout the night, I found excuses for myself to slip downstairs and peek at the dirt where I'd buried the wolfsbane.

There was no apparent rupture in the dirt; nothing to physically see in the darkness from a glossy window with the naked eye. Yet I couldn't keep myself from trying to catch a glimpse of *something* to confirm the plant was still there.

I felt my thoughts morphing, fixed. I was no longer just thinking about the wedding. Instead I was consumed with the growing desire to utilize the wolfsbane Ms. Volkova handed to me, to test its true potential.

I could mix it in his tea, studying his expression with every steady sip.

I started asking myself, *what would happen if I stopped holding the edges and just let it all fall?*

I slipped back into bed, forcing my eyes shut and my breathing pattern to mirror Remmy's. But all night, the thought circled my mind like my hand circling a pot on the stovetop.

In the morning, I slipped outside before the sun rose, digging up the tiny bouquet of wolfsbane, its white flowers now stained with dirt. I carried it inside and gave it a careful rinse, my body moving before my mind had caught up to the decision.

A scent of damp earth still clung to my palms, grounding me more than thought ever could.

Maybe it wasn't curiosity at all. Maybe I just wanted proof that I could choose who lived untouched and who didn't. That I was in control.

In the basement, the mortar and pestle felt heavier than usual. The roots resisted me—fibrous, stubborn—forcing me to grind with more effort than expected. The powder came out uneven, some of it coarse as bark, some as fine as ash. I should have felt triumphant when I bottled it, but the inconsistency unsettled me.

The color was like dried soil, the smell faintly metallic. I tested a trace amount on my tongue, but it left me unsure—harsh, but not overwhelming. Had I measured too little? Too much?

I boiled the water anyway, letting the tea steep eleven full minutes instead of five. The steam curled in pale ribbons, carrying a bitterness I could almost taste without sipping. I added lemon balm, mint, and honey, layering sweetness like curtains over a locked door.

Denver sat in the doorway, ears down, gaze steady.

"It's just tea," I muttered, nudging him with my foot. "You're not the one drinking it."

When Remmy came down, mussed hair and tired smile, I nearly dropped the cup. My palms felt slick, though the porcelain was cool.

"Oh—tea?" he asked.

"I made some. Want a cup?"

He accepted without hesitation. Fingers curled around the mug. Trust dulls the instinct to flinch.

He sipped, humming softly. "Nice. Tastes like something from a retreat—linen clothes, chakras." He laughed, took another sip, then set the mug down half-full on the counter to check his phone.

I froze.

He scrolled, stretched, scratched Denver's head. Talked about his shift. The tea cooled untouched beside him.

At last he took several sips. "Bitter," he said absently, pushing it away. "Maybe the honey's old." Then he kissed my temple, rinsed the mug with casual indifference, and carried on with his morning.

He never asked why his tea tasted different, never wondered what else might be slipping past his tongue.

Upstairs, drawers opened, the TV hummed. Normal life marched on.

I sat in the study with my pen poised, waiting for symptoms, but there was nothing. No headache. No pallor. No fatigue beyond what he carried every morning after a night at the hospital.

My notes stayed blank. The paper warped under my hand, and for the first time, I wasn't sure if the quiet meant safety—or if I'd simply missed the signs.

I'd wasted powder. I'd risked exposure. And for what? Nothing.

Failure clung to me like damp air. Not proof, not even doubt—just emptiness.

I was halfway to rinsing the kettle when I felt it— that shift in the air, the kind that comes before you're seen. The house held its breath.

When I finally turned to the sink, Volkova's face appeared through the screen on the back porch, her voice sharp and low. I was startled even though I saw her. "Brought you some plants—labeled their uses. Freeze what you won't use in two weeks."

Her eyes lingered as she handed me the Ziplocs.

"Be careful with the one labeled widow's milk," she added, her tone making it sound less like advice than judgment.

She stayed a moment longer. Behind me, the clock ticked too loud.

She glanced towards the stove through the slats. "Pretty tea kettle," she said with a nod. Her voice carried the flat weight of memory, like she was reminding me of something I'd already forgotten.

My blood froze.

I said nothing.

"Heats evenly," she continued. The words landed like a test. I didn't know if she was warning me or waiting for me to lie. She turned and held my gaze for a beat too long before disappearing down the step.

Her boots left soft prints in the dirt, trailing off like an unfinished sentence.

Inside, the kettle was still warm. I stared at it until the metal cooled, half-expecting it to speak—to tell me what she already knew.

And maybe she did suspect something between Remmy and me. Some people can smell a secret the way others smell smoke—faint at first, but impossible to mistake once it's in the air.

And once they smell it, they never stop looking for the fire. I only wondered when she'd realize the match was already lit.

# Chapter 4:

# Car Parts

I hadn't done it.

The thought gnawed at me as I gripped the wheel, adrenaline with nowhere to go, buzzing uselessly in my fingertips.

Last night's attempt replayed in my mind like a reel, but there was nothing to hold onto—no symptoms, no confirmation, just Remmy rinsing his mug and moving on with his evening as if I hadn't risked everything.

I replayed the moment he lifted the cup, the way steam curled against his face, how casually he trusted me. And still... nothing. No stagger, no paleness, no proof. Only my own nerves, my own sweat, betraying me.

When he kissed me goodbye that morning, I searched his mouth for any trace of bitterness, any lingering taste that might prove the tea had marked him. But it was just a kiss, ordinary and unburdened, as if the night before had never happened at all.

The failure pressed heavier than success ever could. I knew that if I wanted results moving forward, I couldn't afford hesitation again.

I clicked my blinker on Hennaway Street, forcing my attention back to the road. A box of car parts shifted in the passenger seat—alternator components Remmy had asked me to drop off at Matt's automotive shop.

Matt Kowalski had been Remmy's best friend—the kind who showed up when you needed help moving, who remembered your birthday without Facebook reminders and sent snail mail for holidays.

He would also do anything to protect Remmy.

I'd always found Matt pleasant enough, in the way you find a coworker pleasant—professionally friendly, reliably appropriate, utterly forgettable unless directly engaged.

He was helpful, funny when he wanted to be, and devoted to Remmy with uncomplicated affection. He was someone who'd never had to compete for attention or wonder about hidden motivations.

Most frustratingly, Matt came as a package deal with Remmy. Every major decision had to survive Matt's scrutiny, every plan had to accommodate Matt's schedule, every celebration included Matt's presence.

Bringing the parts to his shop should have been simple, routine. But as I drove toward the industrial district where Matt rented his garage space, irritation pressed tighter with every mile.

The problem with Matt wasn't just his presence— it was his influence. If Matt suggested that someone might not be trustworthy, Remmy would start looking for evidence to support that theory rather than questioning whether the theory itself was valid. He trusted him, possibly more than me.

I pulled into the parking lot, barn cats keeping an eye on me from afar.

Matt was already leaning against his car when I arrived, even though I was ten minutes early. I couldn't read the expression on his face.

"Emily! Perfect timing. I just finished up the transmission work on the Mustang."

"Hey, Matt." I kept my voice even.

I'd never been unkind to Matt, though at times I felt the urge to knock him down a peg or two. It was his insistence on being in our lives, coupled with a lack of awareness that made me pick at my scars—like putting his feet on the coffee table, socks worn from a day's work.

This morning, though, he was in a good mood. He popped the trunk with a flourish and said, "Got you the good boxes, not the dented ones. Don't say I never spoil you."

I snorted. "I'll write you a thank-you card."

"You better. Hallmark, glitter, the whole nine yards."

For a moment, it felt like we were just two people hauling junk, joking like normal friends of a mutual friend might. The kind of harmless interaction that almost made me forget how closely he watched me.

After that, we became lost in conversation about nothing while unloading boxes of car parts and junk. Every few minutes, I'd catch him glancing in my direction.

Matt took a heavy box from me, my hand coming into view. My fingertips were stained with bright fuchsia—the mark of the new specimens I'd recently been digging through from the web.

"Periwinkle?" he muttered, almost to himself. "That stuff stains."

A cool chill ran through my blood. *Madagascar periwinkle*—the plant variety I'd been working with—leaves a light purple residue, no different from a night with messy art supplies.

But he knew exactly what plant I had toyed with by simply peering at my fingers.

My legs went liquid, as if my bones had quickly dissolved.

"New gardening class." I brushed his comment off, changing the subject to preseason trades—something I only knew from Remmy's ramblings at the TV.

His gaze lingered on my hands a second too long, like he wasn't buying my excuse.

He reached for the rag on the counter, tossing it toward me. "Might want to wash up before Remmy notices." The words were casual, but they made me wonder why Remmy would think anything of it.

Matt didn't watch me clean them. He watched whether I would. He wasn't just noticing—he was testing.

I forced my voice steady, but the weight of his silence pressed harder than his words.

When we finished loading the remaining parts into proper containers, I was ready to leave, but Matt lingered by my car in a way that suggested he had something else to discuss.

"You holding up okay?" he asked, staring at his shoes. The question carried more weight than simple politeness usually required.

"I'm fine."

"Good. Because you don't have to be, you know. The wedding stress, all the planning and coordination—it's a lot for anyone to handle."

His tone was gentle, supportive, the voice of someone who wanted to be helpful rather than judgmental. But underneath the concern, I caught something else—evaluation, assessment, the subtle probing of someone who was trying to determine whether intervention might be necessary.

"Thanks, but I've got it under control."

"I'm sure you do." He looked up, giving me a long look that felt like a measurement. "Just remember that Remmy's got people who care about him. People who want to make sure he's happy and safe. I'm sure you do too."

His words carried enough genuine weight to feel like a warning: "People will always look out for him." His stare deepened.

He tapped his phone against his thigh twice, as if considering something unsaid. For one dizzying second, I wondered if he'd already told Remmy, if their silence was another kind of conspiracy.

The words settled into my chest like stones, heavy and indigestible. Matt wasn't just suspicious anymore—he was positioning himself as Remmy's guardian, someone who would protect him from threats. That made him more than annoying; it made him dangerous to everything I'd started planning.

I could barely control the quiver in my lips as the implications of his statement sank in.

If Matt had been paying attention, holding more knowledge of botany than I'd give him credit for, then my margins for error were much smaller than I'd calculated.

What else had he noticed?

"I should get going. Wedding appointment," I stammered, moving toward my car with haste. "Thanks for helping with the cleanup."

"Anytime." Matt stood motionless. He didn't move, just watched me with the patient attention of someone who had ample time.

As I drove away, I caught sight of him in my rearview mirror, still standing where I'd left him, posture stiff as a scarecrow.

I understood now that if I wanted to be successful, I would have to account for Matt's scrutiny. Be more careful about leaving traces, more thoughtful about what residue I might leave behind. He was providing me information, and I could adjust. Information wasn't a threat; it was leverage.

For a moment, I imagined the barn cats circling his feet, patient and watchful, waiting for him to sniff out the weakness he'd already sensed.

Matt wasn't just an obstacle. He was a test—a reminder that perfection meant knowing which weeds to prune. And he was showing me exactly which weeds needed to be ripped from the dirt.

My hands fought to keep the wheel steady.

They had settled by the time I pulled into the neighborhood. The nerves that rattled me earlier, the faint tremor in my fingers, had gone quiet. A date with foreign petals wasn't enough to connect the dots.

The plan had been seamless. Remmy hadn't noticed anything strange in the tea. He had drunk it as though it were any other morning ritual, distracted, barely looking at me. He had no reason to share any details of the night with Matt.

Time would forgive Matt's memory, the periwinkle of my fingertips lodged far into the void. The next dose—the one meant to kill—wouldn't come until the night of the wedding. That window of time stretched before me like a dark promise.

I rounded the alley that cut to mine, passing Ms. Volkova's side yard. I couldn't help but notice a splash of new color.

When I stepped out of my car in the garage, a scent of gasoline and soil from an old bag of potting mix clung to the air. As I closed the car door, curiosity tugged me to the gate between our houses.

She was crouched over her flower beds, pruning shears in her hand, glasses slipping down her nose. Her eyes were sharp despite her age, the kind that seemed to catalog everything and keep it for later.

Her uniform was as dependable as the sunrise: canvas pants smeared with dirt, a faded long-sleeved shirt that looked decades old, and gardening gloves shoved into her back pocket. She looked like she'd grown out of the earth itself, tough and rooted, impossible to imagine anywhere else.

"Morning," I offered, cautious.

"You're late," she said without looking up.

"For what?"

"For noticing the peonies. They were planted this morning. You missed the show."

I leaned against the fence and scanned the garden, searching for them among the ordered chaos. Plants that shouldn't have thrived together spilled side by side, herbs tucked among ornamentals, everything arranged with a logic I couldn't quite decipher.

"I don't know much about flowers," I admitted.

"What do you know?" She didn't look up.

I felt heat in the back of my neck, embarrassed of my lack of response. "Not enough to have anything to repeat."

"The most important lesson? Everything blooms when it's ready." Her shears clicked. "Force it, and the petals fall apart faster."

Her words felt like more than gardening advice.

I looked at her, unsure how to proceed. "Are you implying something?"

"You're not marrying a man," she said finally, meeting my gaze. "You're marrying an idea of one. A story someone told you. I just hope it's a good story is all."

The accuracy stung, sharp as the scent of cut stems. How much had she seen from her side of the fence? From her kitchen window?

I crouched down to her level, pretending to study the flowers but really reading her face.

"How do you tell them apart?" I asked. "The safe plants from the dangerous ones. They all look beautiful."

"Experience," she said. "And remembering what happens when you make mistakes."

"But there are thousands of varieties. How can you keep track?"

She set down her shears, giving me a look sharp enough to cut. "There are thousands of chemicals for chemists to memorize too. What are you really asking?"

Heat rose in my cheeks. "I just meant—what if you don't know something's dangerous? How do you protect yourself from accidents?"

"I just know." Her tone shifted, deliberate now. "And I never share dangerous things with people who can't handle them."

Without warning, she plucked a stem from the bed and held it out. She handed me a mini shrub I hadn't noticed before—white petals edged in bruised pink, waxy against my fingers.

"This one's from the same realm as before," she said. "But the compounds concentrate differently."

I stared at the petals, its shine captivating me. "Poisonous too?"

"Only if you use the roots." She nodded at the bloom in my hand. "The petals are less concentrated. But the roots hold enough cardiac glycosides to stop a heart, if prepared properly."

I froze, the flower suddenly heavier. "That's... very specific knowledge."

"My grandmother believed in knowing all the tools at your disposal," she said, standing and brushing dirt from her hands. "Not just the ones people approve of."

She started toward her porch, walking slow and deliberate, pausing halfway across her fence.

"The roots need drying," she added over her shoulder. "Fresh ones are unreliable. Dried and ground, though, they dissolve clean in hot liquid. Bitter, but honey hides it."

And then she was gone.

I stared at the bloom. Delicate, lovely, yet laced with the potential to kill. It was a grenade disguised as a flower, its pin resting against my fingers, daring me to pull.

Volkova's flowers never wilted into the ordinary. They resisted, threatened, demanded notice. That's what she was really teaching me—not about petals, but about how to be unforgettable.

I thought of Remmy, his smile wide above his breakfast plate. He had even expressed his gratitude. Was that not him asking for more?

His words taunted me: *Tastes like something you'd get at a retreat.*

I thought of our wedding bouquets—roses, baby's breath, flowers chosen to look perfect for six hours before collapsing under the heat. Beauty with no purpose.

This bloom was different. Its beauty asked you to linger, to study. A set of flowers that carried secrets in its roots, waiting for the one bold—or foolish—enough to reach for them.

I carried it inside, laid it on the kitchen counter, and wrapped it in paper towels with surgical neatness. My laptop hummed to life, and in minutes I had matched its image online. *Nerium oleander.* I typed the name carefully into my notes. The letters of its name looked stark and clean on the screen, like a formula scrawled in chalk.

A flicker of memory rose unbidden—science class, the chalkboard, the teacher's looping handwriting. *Experiments require repetition.*

The words had stayed with me long after the chalk dust faded. And as the flower sat in its paper shroud, I felt the old lesson stir again, tempting me.

My first experiment failed. But repetition fixes margins of error.

I catalogued the flower and pressed a couple of its petals into my linen manual.

That evening, Remmy was extra affectionate for running the parts to Matt. His hands found my waist more than once, settling into our usual rhythm of domesticity. I found myself staring at the mini shrub on our windowsill.

It had the kind of beauty that asked you to stay close, to learn its secrets—even as it waited for you, taunting you to take a step too far into knowledge you weren't sure you wanted to possess.

It was thriving in small pots, reaching toward the light with the determination of living things that refused to give up.

I'd researched it, of course. Alkaloid content, preparation methods, historical uses—Victorian women had known things about the Earth we've dismissed as folklore but were really chemistry disguised as myth.

Remmy kissed my neck and opened a bottle of wine without asking if I wanted any. It was a tiny presumption, that we'd share the bottle.

That's what we always did, but it lodged under my skin in a way I couldn't name.

He didn't notice the flower on the windowsill. He never noticed changes to our environment unless they directly affected his comfort or convenience. I could have rearranged the entire kitchen and he wouldn't comment unless he couldn't find something he needed.

Maybe that was why order was my job. Someone had to keep the room safe.

I found myself wondering what Ms. Volkova would have done. *Volkova would have noticed the flowers. Volkova would have asked the right questions.*

"How was your day?" he asked instead, settling into his chair with the wine and his phone, ready to divide his attention between me and whatever emails had accumulated while he was driving home.

"Fine. Productive." Followed by a shrug.

He smiled but shook his head. "You don't have to script every second, Em. You can have a day without being productive."

I watched him scroll through messages, dismissing me.

"I spent some time with Ms. Volkova. She's teaching me about gardening."

"That's nice," he said without looking up. "She seems friendly enough. The woman's probably lonely, living by herself."

Sure, she appeared friendly. But she was deliberate, knowledgeable, someone who understood the difference between appearance and reality.

Someone who could hand you a flower and let you decide what to do with the information that came attached to it.

If he knew what she'd handed me, what rested on the windowsill, fifty yards from a couch that spoke of safety...

The thought alone made me feel dangerous—like the act had already begun, even if I hadn't moved yet.

"She's not lonely," I said. "She's careful about who she lets close to her."

The conversation was over as far as he was concerned, his focus switched to the category of domestic chitchat that didn't require full engagement.

What lingered wasn't the specific knowledge Ms. Volkova had shared, though that sat in my mind like a loaded gun I wasn't ready to fire. It was the casual way she'd offered it, like she knew exactly what I was asking for and approved of the asking. Like she recognized something in me that I was only beginning to see in myself.

The thought stuck with me throughout the night, through a perfectly-prepared dinner, our favorite comfort show, a late-night walk.

Ms. Volkova's confident gaze was burned into my memory.

After Remmy had gone to bed and the house settled into the quiet that made thinking too easy, I took the shrub from the windowsill and examined its flowers closely.

The root system was more complex than I'd expected, branching into tiny fibers that had been working to keep the plant alive, despite being transplanted into an artificial environment.

I could dry it, grind it, test its properties the way Ms. Volkova had suggested. Learn through experimentation rather than just theory. Understand what I was working with before I decided whether I was brave enough to work with it at all.

Or I could throw it away, pretend this conversation had never happened. Go back to planning a wedding that would lead to a marriage, slowly suffocating me in silk and sugar until I was forced to drown out the noise another way.

The choice felt both enormous and simple, like the act of stealing a forbidden fruit.

I wrapped the root carefully in a paper towel and placed it in a small box in my dresser drawer—next to the jewelry I never wore, the letters I'd never sent, the pieces of myself I'd buried but hadn't forgotten.

Not using it, not yet. Just keeping it close, the way some people kept photographs or heirlooms— evidence of possibilities I wasn't ready to abandon.

Not using it wasn't the same as forgetting it, though.

# Chapter 5:

## Refining the Delivery

Remmy never did ask about the tea. I waited for symptoms to come up days after. I catalogued his movements, searched for paleness, for hesitation, for anything that could confirm what I'd done. But there was nothing. Just silence. Just failure.

Maybe the dose was too weak. Maybe he was too distracted. Or maybe I'd been too cautious, letting nerves blunt the edge of what should have been decisive.

Still, I documented it anyway. Even failure had to be recorded.

*First trial: Wolfsbane infusion. Subject compliance: partial. Dose insufficient. No measurable symptoms. Notes: experiment inconclusive.*

The words looked clinical on the page, as if I were logging data for a research lab instead of a kitchen table. But the implication was unavoidable: I hadn't succeeded.

Failure pressed heavier than proof. It demanded correction.

So I planned again. Adjusted dosage. Refined delivery. Shifted method from hot tea to iced—

something he'd drink without thinking, without slowing.

If the first attempt had been a false start, the next one would be undeniable.

I'd spent the intervening time researching tolerance levels, cumulative effects, the possibility that repeated exposure might sensitize rather than inure.

The medical literature was frustratingly vague about alkaloid metabolism in healthy adults, but I'd found enough to support a conservative approach.

This time, I delivered the dose in iced tea on a warm afternoon, when cold beverages would be most appealing. I added a handful of strawberries, plus a sprig of basil and mint to disguise the bitterness. With each strawberry dropped into the water, I watched the condensation trickle down the glass.

"This is perfect," Remmy said, accepting it without hesitation. "Exactly what I needed after that heat."

He gulped it down like water, never pausing to notice the sharpness under the sweetness.

He trusted anything placed in his hand. I knew he trusted me.

He stood at the kitchen counter, scrolling through emails, before wandering to the living room to continue his digital catch-up.

*Ideal: No lingering after-taste, not focused enough to parse texture.*

The effects were subtle, but measurable this time. Mild fatigue he blamed on work. A brief spell of feeling "spaced out" he dismissed as dehydration.

He pushed to standing and stammered, "Time for bed," the words slurring.

He swayed, and I steadied him with a hand on his arm, murmuring comfort while silently noting motor-coordination impairment at T+65 minutes.

I handed him water and lay beside him. Once he slept, I noted the deep unconsciousness of someone whose system was laboring to process unfamiliar compounds. My mind was fixed on his breathing, and I felt the peculiar satisfaction that comes from complete control over another person's experience.

I documented everything.

*Second trial: Iced tea delivery. Half dosage. Onset approximately 50 minutes.*

*Effects more subtle but consistent with expectations. Subject attributed symptoms to external factors.*

*No suspicion detected.*

He was alive because I chose to keep him alive. When he felt well, it was because I chose to let him feel well. It was intoxicating: His comfort, his health, his very survival depended on decisions I made in private, with knowledge he didn't possess, using methods he couldn't detect.

That was the difference. Ordinary wives kept their husbands alive because they had to. I did it because I decided to. That choice made me exceptional.

The more I learned, the more I wanted to explore the outer boundaries of possibility—the difference between a test dose and a therapeutic dose, between temporary discomfort and permanent resolution—between research and application.

The wedding was rapidly approaching, but I no longer thought of the ceremony as an ending. I thought of it as a final exam, the moment when theory would become accomplishment.

The notebook in the crawlspace had grown thick with data, the kind of detailed documentation any serious researcher would maintain. Reading through my notes felt like reviewing the work of someone whose dedication to their craft was both admirable and terrifying.

Someone who had discovered her true calling—and was perfecting it, one dose at a time.

I continued listening to Remmy's breathing in the darkness. His sleep patterns had become as familiar to me as my own, perhaps more so since I'd been studying them. My focused attention matched someone whose plans depended on understanding exactly when he was most vulnerable.

A complicating factor was Matt, whose suspicion felt like a permanent gnat hovering near my ear. But I was approaching a point where observation wouldn't matter anymore. Whatever suspicions Matt was developing, whatever case he thought he was building—it would all become irrelevant once I moved from preparation to action.

The digital clock cast red numbers across Remmy's peaceful face: 3:17 a.m.

His breathing was deep and even, the kind of unconsciousness that came from complete trust in his environment; absolute confidence that nothing in his safe, comfortable world could have any other intentions.

Like someone who'd never been given reason to fear the people who claimed to love him.

He had no idea that the woman lying six inches away had been cataloguing his physiological responses, mapping his vulnerabilities; that I was developing increasingly sophisticated methods for manipulating his body chemistry without his knowledge or consent.

I pressed my ear to the pillow and counted his breaths until my own heartbeat finally slowed to match his rhythm.

But sleep wouldn't come easily. My mind kept circling back to the notebook, to the data I'd accumulated, to the question of what I wanted to do with the expertise I'd developed.

The experiments had been educational, but education without application felt incomplete, like learning a language you never intend to speak.

I took a sip of my own tea, a bitter bite staining my tongue. Static rose in my ears, faint at first, then insistent.

A tuning into a radio station that had been broadcasting just below the threshold of hearing.

A vision surfaced with startling clarity. I wasn't in my bed anymore, wasn't listening to Remmy's trusting breath in the darkness of our shared room.

I was standing in a kitchen that wasn't quite mine, though it could have been. My legs brushed against the table, a widow's table, its surface cleared except for one porcelain mug set carefully in the center. The air smelled of Pine-Sol and roses, like the sweetness of neighbors dropping in with condolences, the cleanliness of a house scrubbed for guests who'd come to offer pity.

I poured something warm into the mug. Not for him anymore—never for him—but for me, for the image it created. My hand trembled just enough to appear fragile, delicate.

In the dream, I could feel the eyes of others watching me: the neighbor across the fence, the friend from church, the grocery clerk with pity in her eyes. All of them whispering the same word: *widow.*

The mug trembled between my fingers. I lifted it anyway, letting its steam curl into shapes—petals, veils, funeral crowns. The taste was metallic, bitter, like pennies or electricity, but I swallowed it as if grief itself could be consumed.

Afterward, the kitchen glowed with false sweetness: syrup, butter, the smell of casseroles cooling in neat rows on the counter. Condolences disguised as meals. Affection disguised as offerings. Every dish was another tribute to my survival, to the myth of my loss.

I sat in that kitchen, surrounded by food and silence, smiling beneath a veil no one could see.

I shot upright in bed, breath coming quick and shallow, heart hammering against my ribs with the force of a dream I hadn't chosen but one I craved all the same.

Denver stirred at the foot of the bed, lifting his head to check whether my sudden movement required his attention. But when I made no further noise, he settled back into sleep with the easy trust of a creature that had never learned to fear the people who cared for him.

All the men in this house trusted me enough to sleep peacefully—the dog at my feet, the man at my side. Neither had learned yet what that trust cost.

The clock now read 4:23 a.m., and Remmy continued sleeping peacefully beside me, undisturbed by my jolt.

I wasn't doing this out of rage or frustration or the need to punish someone for disappointing me. This wasn't about correction or discipline.

This was about research, about performance, about preparing for the role that only tragedy could cast me in.

I lay back down and tried to find sleep in the rhythm of Remmy's unconscious trust.

But the fantasy lingered like smoke: the widow's crown, the whispers of neighbors, the casseroles and lowered voices, the way grief made a woman holy.

Ordinary wives were invisible. Widows were unforgettable. That crown was worth everything.

Volkova wasn't handing me tools. She was handing me the throne.

Tea, flowers, the vessels didn't matter. The lesson was always the same: loss was the surest way to be remembered.

She was right. Ordinary people lived and died unnoticed. But widows—widows became legends.

# Chapter 6:

# Monopoly

The next morning felt like Groundhog Day. Remmy stretched awake the same way, pulling me into him across the blankets.

It was the same domestic ritual—two Sims orchestrating their parallel lives.

That evening we sat at our kitchen table with Matt, a charcuterie board half-eaten between us.

The same Matt who acted suspicious at the shop, noticing my purple fingers—the same Matt whose gaze lingered longer than I could stomach.

Monopoly houses and hotels spilled from a worn velvet bag that had seen better decades, property cards arranged in stacks that revealed each player's strategy. Beers lined the edge of the table, sweating onto the homemade scoreboard, laminated and decorated with outdated Microsoft WordArt.

*Brewsday*, they called it—a ritual that had survived since their college years, evolving from dorm room beer pong to this more sophisticated version of competitive male bonding.

Tonight, the dynamic felt especially pronounced. They'd been trading inside jokes and shared memories while I managed the scorekeeping and refreshed their drinks, performing the role of gracious hostess while calculating property values and mortgage payments in my head.

Matt punched Remmy's arm and peered at me through the side of his eye. "Still working on that Mustang?"

Remmy recoiled, laughing. "Yeah, man. I keep thinking if I fix her up enough, we'll take a road trip— coast to coast. Just us, the car, no deadlines."

Matt nodded without words and glanced at me once more before returning to the game.

The familiar rhythm of their friendship made me feel like an audience member at a show I'd been watching for six years, where all the best lines went to the leads, and I was left to appreciate their chemistry from the sidelines.

"This game's bullshit." Remmy's laugh filled the room. "You get the set of railroad track cards, and it's game over."

He missed the tension entirely, too caught up in dice and beer to notice the air thick with something heavier.

Matt shot back, "Dude, statistically, it's all about Tennessee Avenue."

But I knew it was neither of those options.

It was the carefully crafted decision-making, balancing short-term investments and long-term gains. A game of building the perfect neighborhood, while experiencing the true cat and mouse of someone who seeks the same thing.

I'd already studied it, done the statistics.

Like everything that mattered to me, I studied it.

The game was interrupted by a phone call, something urgent at work Remmy couldn't send to voicemail. He left me alone with Matt.

I peered at the Monopoly board, comparing Matt's side to mine. His money sprawled across the table in careless piles—twenties mixed with hundreds, property deeds scattered like he was too confident in his memory to need organization.

Mine was arranged in neat stacks with paperclips I'd brought from my office, each denomination separated, each property grouped by color. The difference felt symbolic of something larger, though I wasn't sure what.

My Bloody Mary sat mostly untouched beside me, the celery stalk wilting in the tomato juice while Matt worked his way through his second Manhattan.

He drummed his fingers against the rim of his glass, studying me with that too-familiar look I'd learned to recognize and dread.

It was the expression of someone who'd been thinking about you when you weren't in the room, who'd formed opinions about your behavior and was looking for opportunities to share them.

His eyes moved from my face to my hands to the precise arrangement of my game pieces, cataloguing details like he was building a case.

"You ever get tired of it?" he asked, his voice casual but weighted with the kind of false lightness that preceded uncomfortable conversations.

I looked up from counting my rent income. "Tired of what?"

"Keeping everything perfect?" He gestured toward my side of the board, where my properties were arranged in neat rows and my money was sorted with accounting-firm precision. "The house, the wedding planning, this game—everything has to be exactly right. Sounds exhausting to me."

The observation stung because it wasn't entirely wrong. I did prefer order to chaos, systems to improvisation, plans that accounted for contingencies rather than hoping everything would work out somehow.

But the way he said it made those preferences sound pathological, like evidence of some deeper flaw that required intervention.

His tone was light, but his eyes weren't. They held the sharp focus of someone who thought he'd identified a problem that needed solving, a crack in the foundation that might bring down the whole structure if left untreated.

I laughed, the sound sharper and more practiced than I'd intended. "That's just who I am, Matt. Some people like chaos. Some people prefer order."

"Order's one thing," he snapped back, leaning into his chair. "Control's another." He said it like a diagnosis, not a conversation.

The word hit me like a physical blow, sliding under my skin and lodging between my ribs and spine.

*Control.* Ugly when applied to women. When men did it, they were leaders. When women did it, they were controlling. Desperate. Manipulative.

Volkova's words slipped in: *The most dangerous plants look like the safest ones.* Maybe that was true of people too.

Heat started behind my ears, the familiar flush that preceded either tears or violence. "Is this your way of saying I'm a control freak?"

He thought it was about control. But he didn't understand—it was about refusing to live a life so dull no one remembered the details.

He smirked, an expression that managed to be both condescending and affectionate, like he was correcting a child who'd said something adorably wrong.

"I'm saying Remmy's a good guy. The best, really. And he trusts you more than I've ever seen him trust anyone. I just hope..." He paused, swirling what little ice remained in his glass, the sound sharp and deliberate in the silence. "I just hope you're careful with that trust. With him."

The words landed with the precision of a surgeon's scalpel, finding exactly the right spot to inflict maximum damage. Because underneath the concern and the careful phrasing, Matt's message was clear: He thought I was dangerous. He thought Remmy needed protection from me.

His hand hovered over the dice, then set them down. He leaned in, voice lower. "If I ever thought you were controlling him, Emily, I wouldn't just sit here playing games."

"I love him," I said, the words coming out almost too fast, defensive.

"I know you do." His gaze lingered on me for a moment too long, like he was trying to read something written in a language he didn't quite understand.

"I'm just saying—" He studied me too closely. "You've got that look sometimes. Like you're playing a different game than the rest of us."

The air in the room seemed to thicken, pressing against my skin like humidity before a storm. Matt's words hung between us, not quite an accusation but close enough to feel like one.

He'd been watching me, studying my expressions, cataloguing my behaviors and finding them suspicious. The realization that I'd been under surveillance in my own home, by someone I'd thought of as merely annoying rather than threatening, made my stomach clench.

"I don't know what you mean," I said, keeping my voice level despite the adrenaline starting to flood my system.

He smiled then—polite, practiced, utterly unreadable in the way that suggested he'd been rehearsing this conversation. The expression was so perfectly calibrated between friendly and suspicious that it could have meant anything.

If I weren't looking for the tells, I might have missed the slight furrow of his nose, the way his eyes didn't quite match the curve of his mouth.

"Of course not."

The phrase hooked under my skin and stayed there, vibrating like a trapped gnat.

It was the verbal equivalent of a chess move that looked casual but actually put your king in check—a threat disguised as conversation.

Before I could formulate a response that wouldn't sound either guilty or defensive, Remmy's voice drifted back down the hall, bright and effortless as he wrapped up his phone call.

His footsteps approached, and I heard him pause in the doorway, probably sensing the tension that had settled over the room like smoke.

"Sorry about that," Remmy said, sliding back into his chair with the easy confidence of someone who'd never had to wonder if he was welcome somewhere.

"Dr. Peterson had questions about the new rotation schedule. Where were we?"

Matt's demeanor shifted so smoothly it was almost impressive. The suspicious intensity disappeared, replaced by the familiar warmth of friendship, as if the conversation we'd just had existed in a parallel universe that only he and I could access.

"Just talking about Emily's amazing organizational skills," Matt said, reaching for the dice with the casual air of someone who'd been discussing the weather. "She's got this game figured out better than either of us."

But his words sat in the air long after he'd spoken them, clinging like smoke to everything they touched. The echo of them followed me through the rest of the game, through Remmy's cheerful commentary on property values and Matt's increasingly competitive determination to bankrupt us both.

Bile rose in my throat, but I forced my face to remain still, my expression pleasant and engaged.

What exactly was Matt implying? That my organizational skills extended beyond Monopoly and wedding planning? That my ability to think strategically might be applied to areas he couldn't see or understand?

As if he already knew I had something sharp tucked away in my sleeve, waiting for the right moment to use it.

Remmy looked between us, sensing the charged air. "You two okay?" When I smiled too quickly, he frowned. "Huh." He shook it off, dropping back into the game as if his instincts had misfired.

The game continued for another hour, but I barely paid attention to the dice rolls or property acquisitions. My mind was too busy replaying Matt's words, analyzing the subtext, trying to understand exactly what he suspected and how much evidence he thought he had. I'd been so focused on managing Remmy's perceptions that I'd failed to account for Matt's scrutiny, and that oversight felt like a critical strategic error.

Matt's suspicion sat like a stone in my chest, heavy and indigestible. How long had he been watching me this carefully? What exactly had he seen that made him think I was hiding something?

He reached across the table and pulled Remmy's sketchpad closer, flipping through a few penciled tables. "Solid work, man. Can't wait to see it finished." His words lingered in the air, a kind of trust only men give each other. My stomach tightened.

Remmy had pages of honesty in graphite; I had secrets inked in a crawlspace notebook. Guess which one Matt would believe.

I replayed every interaction we'd had over the past months, searching for moments where my mask might have slipped, where my true thoughts might have shown through the careful facade I maintained.

I pondered again about why Matt felt so threatning. It wasn't just that he suspected something—it was that Remmy trusted his judgment completely. They'd been friends since college, had weathered breakups and career changes and family crises together.

If Matt decided I was dangerous, Remmy would listen. That made Matt more than suspicious; it made him a liability that needed to be managed.

When we finally tallied the scores, the irony wasn't lost on me that I'd won while barely paying attention to the actual game. My careful property management and conservative financial strategy had paid off, even while my attention was focused on a completely different kind of strategic thinking.

As I collected my winnings—play money that felt surprisingly substantial in my hands—I caught Matt watching the methodical way I stacked the bills and sorted the properties.

"You're really good at this," he said quietly, his tone suggesting he wasn't talking about board games anymore. "Strategy games, I mean."

His observation felt like both compliment and warning, acknowledgment of a skill that could be used for purposes he didn't want to think about too carefully.

The question was whether I could find a way to neutralize the threat he represented without creating a bigger problem in the process.

I stood at the kitchen window, looking out into the darkness beyond our carefully maintained yard, and imagined a future where Matt no longer mattered. Where his protective instincts couldn't reach me.

Matt himself was part of my planning whether he knew it or not.

# Chapter 7:

# Wedding Dress Shopping

The Monopoly board was still out when I woke up—plastic houses scattered across the coffee table like crime scene markers. I couldn't look at them without hearing Matt's voice again, low and cutting, threaded through what should have been a joke about rent and railroads.

He hadn't raised his voice. He didn't need to. It was the way he slid his gaze across the board, past the dice and paper money, straight to me—like he'd been waiting for the right moment to lay a card I didn't know we were playing with.

It was supposed to be a game, but it hadn't felt like one. Every time he moved his piece, it was like he was moving me. Testing me. Pressing just enough to see where I'd flinch. And when I laughed too quickly, when I smoothed the edges of my voice the way I always did, he only smiled. Not kind, not cruel—just knowingly.

Now the houses and hotels were lying on their sides, and I couldn't shake the feeling they weren't tokens anymore but warnings. Matt had turned a game into a message, and I wasn't sure which part unsettled me more: that he'd done it in front of Remmy, or that Remmy hadn't noticed at all.

I gathered the pieces slowly, one by one, palms damp, as though touching them might trigger something.

Matt had confronted me. Not with words he could be quoted on, but with the kind that stick in your blood anyway.

And the worst part was that no one else would have seen it for what it was. To Remmy, it had been banter over cardboard money. To anyone else, it was just Matt being Matt—competitive, sharp-edged, too invested in a game. But I felt the message land. It was like he'd slipped something under my skin that only I could feel, and now I couldn't stop checking for the wound.

The isolation didn't help. My wedding party consisted entirely of Remmy's family members—his sisters and cousins, none of whom lived close enough to be involved in day-to-day planning, or to notice if my behavior had shifted in ways that might raise questions.

As a result, I found myself standing next to Ms. Volkova in the bridal shop for my final dress fitting, her presence feeling both appropriate and symbolic in ways I couldn't articulate. The saleswoman kept glancing between us with barely-concealed confusion.

The gowns around me looked less like clothing and more like rows of hothouse lilies—identical, white, bred to appear pure, even while rotting at the roots.

Ms. Volkova studied my dress with the same methodical intensity she brought to examining her garden—considering improvements that might not be obvious to casual observers. She was circling my reflection in the three-way mirror with the patience of someone evaluating a rare specimen.

"Something is missing," she insisted.

The dress was beautiful—simple lines that flattered without drawing attention to themselves, fabric that moved naturally rather than requiring careful management. A design that would photograph well under various lighting conditions.

Everything a sensible bride would choose for a wedding that prioritized elegance over noise.

But under Ms. Volkova's scrutiny, it felt insufficient somehow.

Suddenly I noticed the boxiness of the neckline, the way my arms appeared less flattering than normal. Typically, I wouldn't spot such detail or be one to scrutinize, but Ms. Volkova's presence made me sharpen my presence.

She disappeared without explanation, moving through the rows of white gowns with purpose I couldn't interpret. I stood alone on the fitting platform, surrounded by mirrors that reflected versions of myself I barely recognized. I looked less like a bride and more like a specimen bloom, petals arranged for display while the roots stayed hidden, waiting.

Every other bride in those mirrors looked the same. Ordinary, forgettable. I refused to vanish into their white noise.

The irony wasn't lost on me that I was shopping for a wedding dress with the woman who had unknowingly provided nearly all of my botanical education, who had given me flowers that could kill. She fed me information about preparation methods without ever asking what I intended to do with the knowledge she was sharing.

Ms. Volkova reappeared, carrying fabric samples and a look of professional determination that suggested she'd identified the problem.

"Sleeves," she announced, dismissing my bare arms with a wave. "You need sleeves for this kind of ceremony."

The saleswoman looked bewildered. "We don't typically add sleeves to dresses at this stage of the process. The timeline would be very tight, and custom alterations are expensive..."

"I'll make them," Ms. Volkova interrupted, already sorting through lace samples with the confidence of someone who'd done this kind of work many times before. "I have more than enough time for proper sleeve construction."

There was no arguing with that tone. I'd heard it before when she'd handed me dangerous plants with casual authority, the voice of someone who understood exactly what she was doing and expected others to trust her expertise without question.

It wasn't arrogance; it was precision. The kind of precision I'd spent months chasing.

"You don't have to—" I began.

I obeyed because there was nothing else to do. As I pulled the dress over my head in the fitting room, I could hear her voice drifting through the curtain— calm, decisive, every syllable deliberate. She was talking about seam allowances and thread weight, about stability points on delicate lace, the kind of language that revealed decades of practice. The saleswoman was reduced to monosyllables, caught between awe and intimidation.

Volkova's authority filled the shop like a weather system. It was the same energy she brought to her garden: purposeful, exact, faintly dangerous. She didn't just make things—she controlled them, reshaped them until they obeyed.

When I emerged, street clothes back on, the saleswoman was still nodding helplessly as Volkova pinned down the schedule. She didn't smile, but her hands worked with the steady patience of someone who trusted her own vision more than anyone else's approval.

"I'll have more than enough time," Volkova repeated, brushing invisible lint from the lace. "This will be finished."

I made a note to myself—again—to remember how easily she cut through resistance, how quickly she bent people to her timeline without raising her voice.

Walking out into the cold air, the dress bag heavier on my arm than it should have been, I realized something: Volkova wasn't just building sleeves. She was building certainty.

She was giving me proof that even the most rigid systems could be undone, reworked, if you knew where the seams were.

That thought stayed with me all the way home, where Remmy greeted me with an easy grin and an absentminded kiss, like the dress was just another errand checked off. He never thought about seams— only surfaces.

That was his weakness.

I started to garden shortly after returning, inspired by Ms. Volkova's commitment across the fence.

Matt came through the back gate, passing me on his way in to hang out with Remmy.

His gaze lingered just a second too long, a little too sharp.

For a second I wondered whether he was studying me—or whether I was already studying him.

When the dress was ready, I found it carefully arranged on my front porch with a note tucked beneath the plastic garment bag: *Beautiful things require patience. Flowers taught you that. It applies to people, too. —V*

# Chapter 8:

## Silhouette of Order

I'd found myself googling local herbology workshops, a fragment of explanation for my recent infatuation with plants if prompted. A greenhouse a few towns over hosted monthly meetups.

Matt's eyes were watching like a hawk, and I needed to pretend I had my eyes on a different prey. A better explanation for purple fingers and frequent trips to Ms. Volkova's yard.

It helped that the idea of taking a course to deepen my understanding sent a lighting bolt of adrenaline down my spine.

The topic caught my attention: *Seasonal Poisonings: History, Folklore, and Modern Safety.*

I signed up immediately, telling myself it was just research.

But even as I typed my name into the registration form, I knew I was crossing another line—from private experimentation to seeking knowledge I could only use one way. It began to feel out of my control and in my control at the same time.

The confirmation email arrived within minutes, bright and cheerful, as if I'd signed up for a pottery class instead of a tutorial on more efficient ways to kill.

The greenhouse was two towns over, attached to a weathered nursery that smelled like wet soil and fertilizer. String lights were still up from someone's engagement party.

Twenty-three people sat in folding chairs arranged in a rough semicircle, notebooks balanced on their knees. Most looked like suburban gardeners—middle-aged women in cardigans, a few earnest young men with organic coffee cups. Normal people interested in keeping their pets safe from toxic plants.

I wasn't normal people.

My heartrate sped as I crossed the threshold.

The instructor was a narrow woman with clean nails and a teacher's voice that made everyone sit straighter. "Aconitine poisoning presents initially as tingling, then progresses to nausea, cardiac arrhythmia..."

I took notes, my pen moving steadily across the page. Not the theatrical scribbling of someone trying to look engaged, but the careful documentation of someone collecting intelligence.

I swore I saw her eyes narrow in on me.

For a split second I thought she recognized me—not my face, but the part of me that understood.

"We're here to talk about boundaries," she began. "Plants set them. People ignore them." A few polite laughs. Her eyes set on mine again.

She moved jar to jar, telling stories—the shepherd who chewed a stem and slept for three days; the sailor who brewed tea from leaves that looked like something he trusted and never woke up.

Every example landed like a soft threat: innocent mistake, irreversible consequence. The moral was never "don't do it" but rather "know what you're handling."

"Most incidents," she said, "are accidental. Untrained foraging. Mistaken identity. Or," she lifted the jar marked *aconitum napellus* to the light, "curiosity."

The room cooled a degree. I took notes I didn't need.

"Two things matter most," she continued. "Dose and delivery. Aconite, for instance, is more dangerous in concentrated preparations. Heat breaks some alkaloids, but not all. Skin exposure isn't nothing—powder can absorb, especially around the nail beds. Gloves are not a suggestion."

She set the jar down. "Also—symptoms can mimic other conditions. Anxiety. Dehydration. Food sensitivity. People miss what's in front of them because it sounds ordinary."

She passed out a single sheet: historical cases on one side, modern safety tips on the other. At the bottom, a footnote: *Detection is rare outside targeted toxicology. Timing is everything.*

A woman next to me raised her hand. "So if someone ingests a small amount and just... feels off— would they know?"

"Maybe," the instructor said. "But people are experts at explaining their own bodies away."

The class ended with chamomile tea and a peppermint hard candy in a white bowl. I declined both.

I swallowed a lump and gathered the courage to approach Dr. Henley with my prepared question.

"The historical uses are fascinating," I said, nodding toward her display of preserved specimens. "I'm researching family remedies for a genealogy project. My great-grandmother's journals mention something called 'widow's tea'—have you heard of that term?"

Her eyebrows lifted slightly. "Ah, yes. Folk medicine often had... colorful names. Usually referred to concentrated foxglove or sometimes aconitine preparations. Highly dangerous, of course."

"Of course," I agreed. "I'm just trying to understand what she might have been documenting. Are there any academic sources you'd recommend?"

For a moment, she paused—I noticed the crystal of her eyes and I caught a glint that shifted into Ms. Volkova's usual look, as though daring me.

She held my eyes for one moment more before handing me a business card. "Dr. Myrtle Volkov at the university has done extensive research on historical plant toxicology. Tell her I referred you—she's got access to texts that aren't digitized yet."

Myrtle Volkov. Not Ms. Volkova from next door, but close enough to make my pulse skip.

My vision blurred as I reached for the card, its presence both foreign and strangely familiar. The hand that reached for it wasn't mine at first—it was my mother's, steady and knowing. It stretched backward, impossibly, until it reattached to my own arm. I plucked the card with practiced ease, like lifting a toothpick from a jar.

The card was smooth between my fingers, the ink still crisp like it had been printed with me in mind. I could feel Matt's eyes on me even when he wasn't in the room—watching the way I handled this sliver of paper, whether I tucked it into my wallet or dropped it into the nearest trash can.

Keep it, and I'd always know it was there. Proof that someone had given me a way out, or a way to be cornered. Throw it away, and I'd never stop wondering if he'd notice the absence.

The card weighed less than an ounce, but in my hand it felt like evidence. Evidence of what, though— my suspicion, or his?

I folded it once, then again, the edges biting against my skin. Still deciding. Still calculating what looked more natural under the heat of Matt's watch.

I tucked the card carefully into my notebook.

It sat there into the next morning, my hand finding its way to the corners of its cardboard edges enough times to turn it soft. I battled the card in my thoughts over coffee, every label shifting into the card's shape. I saw its green hue in my eyesight as I drove, and I could have sworn the card had continued to howl at me from between the pages.

Two days later, a final beckoning from the card broke my curiosity, and I retrieved its tiny form, white batting spilling out from the edges creased and toyed with.

I found myself in Dr. Volkov's cramped office, surrounded by botanical illustrations and the musty smell of old books. She was younger than I'd expected, with sharp eyes behind wire-rimmed glasses.

"Dr. Henley mentioned you're researching historical family remedies?" she asked, fingers steepled.

I repeated my genealogy story, adding details about wanting to understand the traditional knowledge that had been lost. Dr. Volkov listened with the intensity of someone who rarely had visitors interested in her work.

"The folk preparations were often more refined than people assume," she said, pulling a leather-bound journal from her shelf. "Your great-grandmother might have had access to quite sophisticated botanical knowledge."

She showed me pressed flowers between yellowed pages, pointing out subtle variations in leaf structure that indicated different potency levels.

"This particular specimen," she said, indicating a delicate white flower with blood-red edges, "was used in very specific dosages. Too little had no effect. Too much..." She shrugged. "Well, that's why they called it widow's tea."

I leaned closer, studying the dried petals. "Is this knowledge completely lost?"

"Not completely." Dr. Volkov's voice dropped slightly. "Some practitioners still maintain the traditional methods. For academic purposes, of course."

She pulled out a small amber vial from her desk drawer, holding it up to the light. The liquid inside was the color of old whiskey.

"This is a historically accurate preparation based on a 19th-century formula I've been researching. Museum-quality reproduction, you understand. For my research on how these traditional medicines were actually formulated."

I stared at the vial, my heart hammering. "That's incredible. The historical accuracy must be perfect."

"Oh, it is. Same plant varieties, same preparation methods. Even the same potency as the original." She paused, studying my face. "I sometimes share samples with serious researchers. For educational purposes... I don't have any extra vials of liquid, not yet. But I have the source flower and roots if you really want a sample..." Her voice trailed at the end, like she knew the box she could be slicing open with a knife.

Before I processed my words, I felt myself reaching again for the forbidden fruit. "I would be so grateful for the chance to examine something so authentic," I said carefully. "For my family research."

Dr. Volkov nodded slowly. "I think that could be arranged. Let me prepare a sample for you—I'll include preparation notes based on the historical records."

She grabbed a notebook and started to scribble furiously.

"Mail is more discrete for academic materials," she said, writing my address from my ID the University collected at check-in with careful block letters. "E. Byrd, wasn't it?"

I left her office with my hands shaking and a fresh business card in my wallet. Dr. Myrtle Volkov— "M.V."—had given me exactly what I needed, wrapped in the clean language of historical research.

I tossed and turned all night, haunted by the thought of the envelope wedged into my mailbox. I pictured it arriving in the dark hours, dropped there with the junk flyers and bills. My heart jolted every time I considered the possibility of failure—what if she'd sent it with USPS and the box was too small? What if it was returned to the post office, flagged, logged, waiting for me to claim it under bright lights and prying eyes?

Even the thought of my neighbor rifling through the wrong mailbox made me sweat, their curious fingers brushing over my name before sliding the package back in. I imagined the mailman noticing the weight of it, tilting the envelope in his palm, wondering. Every ordinary sound—the slam of the lid, the creak of the hinge—became unbearable, echoing in my skull before the morning even came.

Every scenario tightened around my chest. Every minute without the specimen pressed against my palm felt like solitary confinement—cut off from freedom, from certainty, from control.

I thought of my mother then, the way she used to speak about patience as though it were a weapon. She could sit for hours, watching water boil, watching people squirm, never flinching. I had never learned that kind of stillness.

By morning, I couldn't bear the waiting. The air was wet with drizzle, a steady grey pressing down from the sky. Sunday had the weight of a bruise, the street hushed as though it knew something I didn't want spoken aloud.

When I opened the mailbox, my pulse stuttered. As if it was delivered by pigeon, the sample had already arrived. The package had a date labeled thick on the top, only yesterday, the ink on the stamp still wet.

No tracking slip, no carrier mark, just my name on one side like it had grown there overnight.

The padded envelope lay wedged between grocery coupons and a postcard from the Fergusons' niece. My name—E. Byrd—was printed in sharp black type.

No "Black." No married name. Just mine.

The name that would soon belong to another life. On report cards. On leases. On documents I might one day burn. Seeing it there was like overhearing my own voice in another room—familiar, disembodied, slightly wrong.

My fingers trembled as I slid the envelope into my tote, as if hiding contraband. It throbbed there with a strange heat, a clock ticking only I could hear.

The park was the only option. Close enough to reach without drawing attention, quiet enough on a damp morning to give me cover. There were corners there—alcoves of brick and vending machines—places to crouch unseen. I couldn't bring the package home, not yet. Too many eyes, too many questions. If I wanted to open it, to breathe for a second without feeling the walls listen, the park was the only place to hide.

Each step toward the park sharpened the ache to look at it, to tear it open right there on the sidewalk. The tote felt alive against my hip, stinging, insistent, as if it were the one leading me forward. I wanted to give in, to see, to know—but eyes could be anywhere.

I scanned the street for joggers, for dog-walkers, for anyone who might glance too long. Even the empty windows seemed to tilt toward me, curtains breathing in and out as if the houses themselves were witnesses. A drip from the gutter behind me sounded like footsteps. My throat tightened at every shadow, convinced it was human-shaped.

By the time I arrived, the sense of being watched had clung so tightly to my psyche that I ducked into a shadowed corner near the bathroom. The brick wall caught at my shirt as I leaned back. The drizzle tapped against the vending machine's tin siding, the only sound besides the wind.

My hand hovered over the envelope, fingers trembling as if it were a live wire. A dozen reasons to wait flickered through my mind—go home, find scissors, steady yourself—but they were drowned out by hunger, raw and urgent. I felt my pulse in my throat, in my ears, every beat telling me the same thing: now.

I tore the package open, feral with greed. Inside—a slender glass vial, filled with roots and petals the color of amethyst. I lifted it, saw my reflection warped and upside-down in its reflective glass curve.

I expected to see myself, but what reflected back was a stranger's mouth, a stranger's eyes—unrecognizable. For a heartbeat, the distortion shifted, and my mother's pale eyes stared back at me, cold and certain, the way they used to when she asked me to watch her work. The echo vanished as quickly as it came, leaving only my own blurred features.

I swallowed audibly, shaking the vision away. My focus dropped to the envelope again, to the paper tucked inside.

A folded note read:

*Dissolves in liquid. Slow onset. Effects within 12−18 hrs.*

Possibilities bloomed in my mind, hot and dizzying. The weight of the world—contained in glass no bigger than my palm.

"Em?"

The voice snapped me back. Too close.

I fumbled the note, shoving it into my tote. My grip slipped, nearly dropping the vial.

Matt stood a few feet away, sunglasses shoved into his hair, coffee cup steaming in his hand.

His eyes flicked to my tote. To my hands. To me.

"Hey," I said, voice too thin.

A raw scratch split across his knuckle—the sort you earn from meddling where you shouldn't. I couldn't decide if that made him feel closer to me or further away.

"You okay?" he asked.

97

"Yeah," I lied, too quickly. "Just... clearing my head."

Matt didn't move. His weight stayed planted, his gaze pinning me before sliding, deliberate, to the tote at my side. The silence stretched. I felt it as pressure, like the wall itself was pushing me forward into him.

His eyes narrowed, studying, cataloguing—then he remembered to smile, and the shift was almost worse.

"I'm heading to the bakery," he said, tone light but too casual, too placed. "Want a croissant?"

I shook my head and tried to steady my voice. "Still have wedding stuff to finish."

His smile faltered at the edges, never touching his eyes. "Of course. Just a few more days."

The words weren't reassuring. They were a countdown.

I peeled myself off the wall, mortar grit clinging to my shirt. Passing him felt like slipping past a guard post. My pulse hammered, every nerve alive with the sense that he'd seen more than I wanted him to.

At the corner, I couldn't resist glancing back.

He was still watching. Hawk-like.

Not curious. Calculating.

Like he had his own set of notes, and I had just given him another page.

The thought followed me long after I passed him, digging in like a splinter. If Matt was already watching for signs of suspicious behavior, I would have to be even more careful about timing, dosage, and the appearance of normalcy.

His comment about my stained fingers had revealed a level of attention to detail I hadn't anticipated, and his warning about protecting Remmy had transformed our relationship from merely annoying to actively threatening. It meant he wasn't just noticing me—he was positioning himself as Remmy's guard, and by extension, my enemy.

I had slipped into a quiet corner, scanning the space before curling my fingers around the vial again, this time inside the tote.

A tremor of doubt prickled my skin. Thoughts drowned me with a wave of nausea.

My mind shifted to the back of my throat where something heavy lingered—not sadness or dread, but something closer to anticipation mixed with the metallic taste of adrenaline.

The feeling reminded me of standing at the edge of a diving board as a child, that moment when your body knows what you're about to do before your mind catches up to the decision.

Except I wasn't a child anymore, and what I was contemplating wasn't a harmless plunge into chlorinated water.

I'd already researched the white flowers with blood-red edges that Ms. Volkova had given me, cross-referencing multiple sources until I understood their alkaloid content. I poured into their historical applications, hours spent leaning into the desktop, studying their modern toxicological profiles.

All I needed now was practical experience—more roots to grind, to test, to transform from theoretical knowledge into applied science.

I carried the vial home like contraband, pulse jumping at every pair of headlights that swept past me. In the basement, beneath the weight of old holiday boxes and a pile of junk for donation, I found a place to hide it—a gap behind a crate marked *Art Supplies*, a spot Remmy would never bother to touch.

The air down there was close, heavy with damp concrete, and I couldn't stay. I climbed back upstairs, restless, and slipped out to the yard, gulping the cool drizzle like medicine. The night pressed in quietly around me, except for the faint, persistent glow across the yard.

I could see a single light glowing in Volkova's kitchen. She kept late hours, I'd noticed, often moving about her routines when the rest of the neighborhood had long gone still.

Perhaps insomnia was common among people who carried dangerous knowledge—cause and effect, action and consequence—that others preferred to ignore.

I was a broken record. Over and over the words repeated like a song stuck in my head: *This is wedding stress.*

I told myself anyone would feel off with a countdown clock taped to their ribs. That was the line I kept chewing until it softened enough to swallow.

But it wasn't the truth. Lies can sit sweet on the tongue if you say them often enough, but that doesn't make them true.

Two times. That was the number that had lodged under my skin like a burr.

Two trials—each one small, neat, contained. No drama, no hospital, no lasting harm. First, nothing. Then, merely a headache that looked like a normal headache. A wave of fatigue that a normal person would attribute to bad sleep. A little disorientation that could have been dehydration, screen time, the wrong shoes. All of it plausible. All of it forgettable.

My notes were exact to my memory. I had been excellent at this.

And it had begun to feel like too much.

The house had gone to bed without me. Remmy's even breathing—four, five, six—came through the cracked bedroom door in a tide. Denver had claimed the cool of the hallway tile, one ear cocked toward any sound that mattered.

After checking on them I left them there and slipped back outside, barefoot onto the back steps where the wood still held the day's heat. The air had that blue, lake-cold smell it gets under the summer sky.

Across the fence, Ms. Volkova's yard was a silhouette of order: stakes set at exact angles, twine like staff lines holding the plants to a tune only she could hear. A single lamp burned in her kitchen window.

I thought of the things she kept in that house, and the things she kept to herself. Of the way she could cut a stem in the dark without missing. Of how she'd soon grow suspicious of my overinterest in her garden. I stood there long enough for my toes to go numb and for the last mosquito to give up on me.

Long enough to say it out loud—quiet, to the fence: "No more trials." Saying it aloud made my ribs loosen a fraction. The words didn't come out noble or sad; they came out practical. A decision about inventory. About risk management. About the kind of woman I was willing to be when the light came back on.

Inside, I made for the kitchen table because that was where you go to make rules you plan to keep. The table had learned our rhythms: budget nights, guest lists, recipes; the occasional fight conducted at a whisper so the neighbors wouldn't become part of it.

I sat and let my hands find something to do. When they couldn't, they found the pile of mail.

It wasn't snooping, I told myself. Somebody had to sort the stack—menus, catalogs, envelopes that pretended to be personal and weren't. I made neat piles because order feels like virtue even when it's camouflage.

Remmy's name appeared in the middle of the stack, printed in a bar-coded font that belonged to hospitals and bills. The envelope was heavier than the rest, the paper with that chalky weight that says "official." My first thought was insurance. My second thought was: *don't.* My third thought won, because I am exactly who I am.

I slid a butter knife under the flap and lifted it cleanly, the way you lift a bead off a string when you know it will roll. Inside: two pages. A letterhead from the clinic he used when he didn't want to page someone from work. Half checkboxes, half narrative. The kind of document meant to sound calm even when it says something you don't want it to say.

*SUBJECTIVE: Patient reports intermittent headaches, lightheadedness, "brain fog," and stomach upset. First symptom appeared "around 1-2 weeks ago". Sleep disturbance alternating with nights of "out cold" deep sleep. Denies chest pain, shortness of breath. No recent fevers. No known exposures. "Feels off."*

I had to set the page down just to keep my hands from curling it.

*OBJECTIVE: Vitals within normal limits. Exam unremarkable. Neurological screen normal. Basic labs deferred per patient preference; encouraged hydration, regular meals, decreased caffeine.*

I felt the rise and fall of my chest. The words started to morph together.

*ASSESSMENT/PLAN: Likely stress and anxiety-related symptoms. Discussed sleep hygiene and stepwise management. Provided mental health resources. Follow-up PRN.*

There was a tiny list at the bottom—names of therapists, a support group for residents, a QR code to a guided breathing app. I stared at the code like it might blink back.

The rest of the paperwork included general medication information and warnings about medications Remmy would never take. I almost missed the note on the backside of the form, the word *friend* catching my eye.

My mouth ran dry as I scanned the page. The paperwork may have been blunt in its summary, but what it implied pressed harder than the words themselves.

*ADDITIONAL SUMMARY: Subject presented stress and anxiety-related symptoms. Patient accompanied by a friend whose presence complicated the exam. Said friend insisted on unnecessary diagnostic tests, including toxicology, which are not within the scope of this office. Provider noted concern over potential undue influence. Possible caregiver pressure or Munchausen by proxy; relationship dynamic warrants monitoring.*

I pressed my thumb hard into the margin until the paper dented. Then I read it again. And again, slower, measuring what had just shifted.

Matt had forced Remmy to see a doctor. Remmy had described what he felt when he drank the tea. He had used the words I had written next to times in my notebook: headache, fog, sleep.

My eyes stuck on the phrase *complicated the exam.* It wasn't just that Matt had been there, hovering like a shadow in a room that should have belonged to Remmy alone. It was that he'd demanded tests—my tests. The very ones that would have pulled the curtain back and revealed everything I'd worked so carefully to keep invisible.

And then the line that knifed clean through me: *Possible caregiver pressure or Munchausen by proxy.*

The words weren't mine, but they might as well have been. The doctor hadn't written *Emily.* He'd written the suspicion in Matt's voice, the doubt in his eyes. If anyone else read this note, they'd see exactly what he wanted them to see: me, orchestrating symptoms, weaving sickness around Remmy like a shroud only I could control.

The word *Munchausen* echoed in my ears like an accusation I'd been waiting my whole life to hear.

But they had given him what the world typically gives to women who admit to being human: a neat bundle of resources and the reassurance that he wasn't broken—just tired, stressed, fixable. They had told him this would pass if he slept enough, if he breathed properly, if he learned to "receive care." Remedies with nothing sharp on them.

I should have felt absolved. If a physician could stand in front of these symptoms and call them ordinary stress, then no one was going to go hunting for something extraordinary. The cover was perfect: a man with too many hours and not enough rest. Statistics were on my side.

That thought didn't settle like I wanted it to, though. Because there was still Matt to deal with.

Remmy hadn't told me he went. He hadn't told me he and Matt were discussing the aftermath of the trials. He hadn't brought the letter home and placed it on the table for us to read together like a map. He had folded it into an envelope and stuck it under the grocery circulars, as if the act itself embarrassed him.

I folded the paper back into its envelope, fingers trembling, pulse in my ears. It wasn't just Remmy's health in question anymore—it was my credibility. My future. Matt had managed to plant doubt where it mattered most: in a doctor's file, stamped and permanent.

*No more*, I told myself again, the conviction final. Not as a strategy. As a rule that would keep whichever parts of me still believed I was a good person.

I looked around the kitchen like the room might have advice. If Matt was watching, he wouldn't need a diagnosis. He'd need a paper trail. This was one.

I didn't intend to give him the satisfaction of finding it on top of the pile. I also didn't intend to throw it away and create a different kind of evidence. I did the thing that had saved me more than once: I split the difference.

I carried the envelope to the pantry, pulled down the binder that held warranty cards and appliance manuals, and tucked the letter inside the section for the smoke detectors—boring enough to repel curiosity, specific enough that I'd remember. Not destroyed. Not displayed. Waiting in a place no one checks unless they have to.

Back at the table, the room refused to change with me. The clock over the stove clicked, unhelpful. The business card in the takeout drawer—the one that wasn't quite Ms. Volkova—throbbed in my head. The little sachet in my cosmetics bag sat upstairs like a dare I'd already declined. I could feel it without touching it. I could feel the way my fingers knew the motions by now. Both practice and perfect have their own gravity.

"No more," I said again, to the glass of water I hadn't realized I'd poured. "For real."

I didn't pour anything down a drain. I didn't stage a purge. I simply moved the bag deeper into the closet and closed the door like a person learning to walk past a bakery without going in. It wasn't a victory banner; it was a habit I would reinforce tomorrow, and the day after that.

Back outside, the square of light in Volkova's window had gone dark. The yard had returned to outlines and intention, a sheet of black stitched with wire and twine. I tried to imagine what she would say if I told her: *I'm done.* She would probably nod once and say nothing, the way people do when they recognize a decision they can't make for you. She appreciates directness and clarity. I had given myself both.

When I came back down the hall, Denver lifted his head and thumped his tail once before deciding I wasn't worth the effort. In the bedroom, Remmy shifted and mumbled a word I couldn't catch. His hand slid across the sheet until it found the place I usually occupy. I fit myself into it and let the bed take my weight like it had been waiting.

Two times.

A number is only a number until you decide it is the edge of a map.

*I can live inside this version,* I told myself. The one where I stopped while I still had a choice.

In the morning, I would put the packet of mental-health numbers on the fridge with a magnet and pretend he'd left it there. I would ask him, casually, if he wanted to try the breathing app as a joke, then download it for both of us. I would make coffee that tasted like coffee and hand him a mug without watching the clock.

I fell asleep counting his breaths, surprised when the number soothed. Somewhere between sixty and seventy, my last clear thought was the simplest: If there's no return address, there's no trail.

That had been my comfort with the envelopes, with the nameless packages, with the brown paper that knew how to keep a secret. But gardens have addresses, and kitchen tables do, too. You can be found. You can be seen.

*No more*, I promised the dark once more—until morning.

# Chapter 9:

# Date Night

Last night's discoveries still clung to me like smoke. The paperwork, the doctor's words, Matt's fingerprints pressed into the margins of my life whether I invited them or not.

I'd folded the summary and hidden it where Remmy would never stumble across it, but the phrases still ran through my head on repeat: *complicated the exam... possible undue influence... Munchausen by proxy.*

I promised myself then and now—no more poison. No more tests. I'd carry the secret weight of what I'd already done, but I couldn't risk another slip, not with Matt circling closer each day.

The house was too quiet without them. Their voices—Remmy's light, Matt's heavier—had followed each other out the door this morning after raiding our eggs and hashbrowns, leaving me with only the silence and the faint smell of soap from where Remmy had shaved in the upstairs bathroom.

I told myself I should use the time wisely. Normal things. Things wives did when their husbands and best friends were out running errands, picking up supplies, doing whatever men thought filled the hours before a wedding.

So I opened the fridge and pulled a mixture of ingredients that weren't spoiled or unpackaged onto the counter. Shredded chicken, iceberg lettuce, and all the best ingredients to craft Remmy's favorite cobb salad.

My hands moved automatically, cracking shells, slicing the pieces even, dicing red onion into neat cubes that stained the cutting board. The smell rose sharp and clean, almost medicinal.

I wanted to be the picture of domestic bliss to present to Matt, to reset the scene he's crafted in his mind.

A wife in her kitchen. A dog underfoot. Lunch waiting on the stove. Not a woman who had scrubbed a mortar and pestle three times last night, rinsing suds down the drain like a crime scene cleaned too quickly.

I laid the skillet on the burner for warming the chicken, letting the oil hiss and pop. My reflection wavered in the pan's surface—warped, bent at the edges, like someone I almost recognized.

"I promised myself," I whispered as I spread the chicken onto the pan with a wet sizzle. "No more."

But even as I said it, I could picture the vial in its hiding place, cool glass against my palm, whispering its promise.

I heated the chicken carefully, plating it with a precision that felt more like ritual than cooking. When I stepped back to look at the finished dish, the thought came unbidden: *See? Normal. See? You can stop.*

And yet, under it all, the awareness lingered— Matt's eyes on me, even in his absence. He'd be with Remmy now, talking, laughing, maybe planting questions I'd never hear until they came back to me, sharpened.

But there was no return address on the package. No evidence beyond what lived in the soil of Ms. Volkova's garden.

That thought soothed me, even as it terrified me.

The chicken cooled as I sat at the kitchen table, fork untouched. Denver settled at my feet with a sigh, his warm weight pressing against my ankles. I envied him—his whole world was a bowl, a walk, a nap. No vials hidden, no neighbors with arsenic in their soil, no men circling her like vultures dressed as guardians.

Tracing circles on the condensation ring left by my glass, I imagined the ink bleeding across paper if I'd written down everything I'd done. I promised myself

I'd never open that notebook again. I'd bury the past where it couldn't be exhumed.

The sound of tires on gravel snapped me back. A car door slammed, then another. Laughter drifted in, muffled but close—Remmy's bright, boyish, Matt's lower, steadier. I froze, listening as if the walls could translate their words.

I rose quickly, scraping the chair legs across the floor. I moved to slice lemon for the water pitcher, spritzing the lemon by pressing the rind, squirting juice slightly onto the floor so the smell would meet them first, proof that I'd been "normal" in their absence.

The front door opened, marking the start of my performance. Remmy's footsteps in the hallway, but not alone—Matt's deeper voice following, carrying the easy confidence of someone who'd never questioned his welcome in our home.

All according to plan.

"We'll catch up in a sec," Remmy called toward the kitchen, where I was stirring the pitcher with a wooden spoon. "Just going to grab a quick shower."

I heard his footsteps on the stairs, leaving me alone with Matt, the exact person whose presence piqued my paranoia. The silence stretched between us, loaded with the weight of suspicions neither of us had articulated directly.

Matt lingered, his hips against the counter, shoving his hands deep in his jacket pockets. His shoes were still on despite Remmy's standing policy about removing footwear in the house. His posture suggested someone who was preparing to leave quickly, who didn't want to get too comfortable or stay too long.

"You okay?" I asked, closing the notebook I'd been writing in and sliding it beneath a stack of wedding magazines with casual precision.

He gave me a half-smile that didn't reach his eyes. "Yeah, just tired. Long week. Think I'm actually going to head out."

"You sure? I was about to start dinner. There's plenty—"

"Rain check," he said, already backing toward the door with the careful movements of someone who'd made an uncomfortable decision and didn't want to be talked out of it. "Tell Rem I'll call him tomorrow."

And then he was gone, leaving me with the distinct impression that he'd seen something he didn't want to stay around to analyze further. The notebook, perhaps, though I'd moved it quickly enough that he couldn't have read any of the contents. Or maybe just the general atmosphere of the house, the sense that something had shifted in ways he couldn't identify but didn't like.

Twenty minutes later, Remmy reappeared looking refreshed and relaxed, hair still damp from the shower, wearing clean clothes that made him look younger and more approachable than he had in weeks.

"Where'd Matt go?" he asked, glancing around as if his friend might be hiding in the living room or kitchen.

"He said he was tired. Decided to head home early."

"Huh." Remmy's brow furrowed slightly. "That's not like him. He was looking forward to trying that new beer I picked up."

I shrugged, trying to project the kind of casual disinterest that would discourage further investigation. "Maybe he wasn't feeling well. People get burned out this time of year."

Remmy accepted the explanation with a nod, his attention already shifting to other concerns. "Speaking of people who might be burned out—I ran into Thomas Clearwater at the hardware store. He's available for the wedding if we want to switch DJs."

My pulse stumbled over the casual way he'd dropped this information, as if changing a major vendor shortly before the wedding was a minor adjustment that didn't require consultation or discussion.

"You changed the DJ?" I kept my voice level despite the adrenaline that had started flooding my system.

"I didn't change anything yet. But Thomas offered, and it would mean a lot to my dad. They go way back— Thomas played at my parents' anniversary party, did my cousin's wedding last year." Remmy was already moving around the kitchen, pulling a soda from the refrigerator with the confidence of someone who assumed his reasoning was sufficient justification. He didn't even motion towards the pitcher of lemon water.

All the hours I'd spent researching DJs, comparing packages, reading reviews, negotiating contracts, and coordinating with the venue coordinator flashed through my mind in rapid succession. The carefully constructed timeline I'd developed, the specific equipment requirements I'd communicated, the playlist we'd spent weeks perfecting—all of it potentially meaningless if he decided to hand the job over to someone else without consulting me.

"You want to change the entire setup?" I asked, my voice foreign.

"It's not that different. Thomas has all the same equipment, probably better speakers, actually. And he knows the venue—he's played there dozens of times."

Remmy's tone suggested he was being reasonable, practical, solving a problem I hadn't even known existed. "Don't worry about it. It's all good."

But it wasn't all good. My chest tightened with frustration that had been building for months, fed by accumulated small betrayals and dismissed preferences.

This wasn't about DJ selection—it was about the systematic erosion of my agency in decisions that were supposed to be collaborative, the gradual transformation of "our" wedding into "his" wedding with my input relegated to decorative details that didn't really matter. A ringing started against my right eardrum.

"I already confirmed everything with the other service," I said, fighting to keep my voice steady. "The contracts are signed, the deposit is paid, the timeline is coordinated with catering and photography."

"I thought I was helping." He reached for my hand with the gentle expression he used when he thought I was overreacting to reasonable suggestions. "Thomas quoted me a price that's actually lower than what we're paying now, and the quality will be better. It's a win-win."

I stepped back before he could touch me, unwilling to be soothed when what I needed was to be heard. His hand hovered, useless, falling back to his side as though he'd realized too late that comfort wasn't what I wanted from him.

For a moment, the air thickened, and Remmy's boyish face—so open, so eager to smooth things over—blurred into another. My father's face. The same soft pleading at the corners of his mouth, the same helplessness in the eyes of a man who never understood the storm he was married to.

And worse, in the cold silence that followed, I recognized myself in her. The sharpness in my voice, the way I held my ground not just to protect myself, but to dominate the space. My mother's anger lived in me like marrow, and in that instant, it rose to the surface.

"You walk in here, announce that you want to change a major vendor, and I'm supposed to be grateful?" The words came out thinner than I'd intended, but the anger underneath was unmistakably sharp.

His expression shifted from patient understanding to defensive confusion. "I didn't announce anything. I said Thomas was available if we wanted to switch. I was trying to give you options."

But that wasn't how it had sounded. It had sounded like a decision that had already been made, a conclusion I was expected to endorse rather than a choice I was being invited to consider.

Remmy put his hands up, surrendering. "Okay, I'm sorry. You're right. I'll let him know it's a no."

My pulse drummed hard enough to blur the edges of his face. Then, like a trick of the light, the image shifted. My father's shadow thinned, and it was only Remmy again—Remmy with his open hands, waiting, his mouth pressed tight in that way he did when he didn't know whether to comfort or retreat.

The rage didn't vanish with the illusion. It only reoriented, finding its target in the man in front of me who looked like Remmy but had, for one dangerous second, carried my father's face.

I continued washing the dishes and tried to swallow my rage. How could Remmy think he was helping by making a major change? Whose shoulders does he think the follow-through will fall on?

"Thank you," I forced. "Wedding stress is—a lot."

But it wasn't wedding stress. It was the urge to slip poison in his tea, to break my promise to myself—to speed up the narrative I'm close to tasting.

Remmy approached me, slipping his arms around my waist, kissing my neck. "I love you, Emily. I see how hard you work."

He had no idea.

Remmy continued apologizing for trying to switch the DJ, sprinkling me with nauseating gestures. Kisses on the neck, expensive gifts I didn't need, and reassurance I didn't seek.

"Wear something nice," he said, kissing my forehead like he was about to board a plane.

I stood in front of the mirror longer than I needed to. The yellow sundress hugged my shoulders softly, flaring just enough at the hips to feel playful. I let my hair fall loose. Lip gloss, not lipstick. The kind of effort that said: *I'm relaxed. I'm trusting you.*

But my reflection didn't buy it. The girl in the glass still carried the echo of my father's face stamped over Remmy's apology, a reminder that the line between then and now wasn't as thick as I wanted it to be.

I leaned in closer, searching for the cracks—anger lingering in the eyes, the faintest tension at the jaw. She didn't look trusting. She looked like someone rehearsing for war and trying to call it peace.

Downstairs, I could already hear him moving— whistling, grabbing his keys, calling out some ordinary reminder that belonged in a sitcom, not in the house where I kept vials tucked behind vinegar bottles. And I wondered, not for the first time, if this was how my mother had felt too: layering charm and cosmetics over a plan, waiting for the right night to test the balance between forgiveness and control.

When I left the mirror, the sundress swayed easily around my legs, but it felt heavier than it should have—like it knew what I was about to carry into the rest of the day.

Denver watched us from the window, paws on the sill like a child seeing his parents off to prom. We drove with the windows down. I reached over and tucked one behind his ear, and he gave me that crooked grin that still made me feel sixteen.

But somewhere between the stoplight and the turn onto Main, I caught him staring out the window like he was somewhere else entirely. His fingers tapped the steering wheel in an uneven rhythm, not to the music—to something in his head.

When I asked what he was thinking, he smiled too quickly. "Nothing."

He parked near the riverwalk and pulled a reservation card from his jacket like it was a lottery ticket.

"Dinner first," he said. "Then adventure."

The reservation card felt less like romance than choreography. He'd planned this comfort. Even the way he pulled my chair out felt timed. Controlled. It made me wonder if I'd ever surprised him at all—or if he'd always been two steps ahead, arranging my reactions like furniture.

The restaurant was one of those hidden bistros where the menu changes nightly and the tables wobble no matter how many coasters you wedge beneath. We sat in the back corner, candle flickering between us, and shared a bottle of red that made everything feel cinematic.

He ordered the duck. I got pasta. We split dessert, even though I claimed I didn't want any.

For two hours, I forgot. I laughed so hard my cheeks ached. He made a joke about the table next to us— something about the man's Bluetooth earpiece being surgically attached—and I nearly spit water onto the bread plate.

After dinner, we walked down to the water. The air was cooler now, and he offered me his jacket even though I didn't need it. He always did that. I always took it.

We found a quiet bench near the river and passed a joint between us like we used to. The burn of it calmed me. We talked about the future—not in abstract, but in detail: what kind of fireplace we wanted. Whether Denver should get a sibling. The cabin he kept sketching on napkins.

He made me promise I'd let him hang a canoe from the ceiling beams, and I agreed even though I hated the idea.

Everything felt light. Real.

For a second, I even forgot the experiments. Forgot that at home, hidden behind the flour bin, there was a page in my planner that read more like a lab log than wedding                                                        notes.

Then he stood up.

"Wanna keep walking?"

I nodded, still warm from the wine and the glow of the lights, and followed.

We strolled for another few blocks, arms brushing occasionally. The air smelled faintly of sugar from the gelato stand up ahead. My chest felt loose, like I could float all the way home.

Then he slowed. His hand dropped from mine. The change was small but immediate—like a record skipping mid-song.

His posture stiffened. "Let's turn back," he said suddenly.

"What? We just got here."

He smiled quickly, but it was the kind of smile people wear when they want you to stop asking questions. "I just realized how late it's getting. You said you had an early morning tomorrow, right?"

"No?"

"Still... I think we should head back."

I glanced down the street. Nothing about it felt dangerous. Enjoying it felt like leaving fingerprints at the scene. Fairy lights strung between brick buildings. A couple laughing so loudly they turned heads.

Nothing strange—except Remmy.

And me, suddenly aware of the weight of my own smile, like my face was performing for a camera I couldn't see.

He kept glancing over his shoulder, like he was checking for the time on something invisible.

"Okay..." I said slowly. "Did something happen?"

"No, no," he said too quickly. "It's nothing."

The denial landed flat.

Just as I started to follow, a voice cut across the sidewalk.

"Remmy? Yo!"

A man approached from the direction we'd just come. He wore a hoodie with DJ CLEARWATER in bold block letters. Two coffees in one hand, like he was on his way back to someone.

"Man, I wasn't sure that was you!"

Remmy froze—not in surprise, but in recognition.

The man turned to me, easy smile in place. "You must be Emily. Heard a lot about you."

125

He held out a fist for a bump. I hesitated, then tapped it. His knuckles were cold from the paper cups.

"Good to meet you," he said. "Thanks again for the gig. Seriously, bro—when you reached out last minute, I didn't think it would work out. Appreciate the trust."

My stomach dropped.

I noticed up close that Tommy's T-shirt saw one too many washes.

"What's up, man?" Remmy said nervously, like he was speaking through his teeth.

"I know exactly what to play. I found your old Spotify, and don't worry—this will be the best wedding you've been to."

Remmy looked like he was about to cry, tears pooling in the corners of his eyes. A small revenge.

"No problem, man. Glad it worked out."

The man winked at me, turned, and disappeared into the crowd.

The sound of his footsteps faded, but the silence he left behind stuck to my skin.

I didn't speak. Not when Remmy said, "Let's go," like he hadn't just detonated a bomb in front of me. I trailed behind him, the name looping in my head like bad hold music.

Not when I followed him to the car, my heels clicking too loudly against the pavement; not in the passenger seat, staring out at the streetlights blurring past the glass.

"I can explain," he said as we merged onto the highway.

I stayed silent.

"I reached out because my dad asked, and I haven't had the heart to tell him we changed our mind."

Nothing.

"Em—I'm going to tell him."

I turned my head slightly toward him.

"When?"

"Soon," he continued. "He's been a family friend for so long, it's hard to tell him no."

"You lied."

"I didn't lie. I just... haven't done it yet."

"That's not better," I said. My voice stayed calm, but my fingers dug into the seatbelt strap.

He sighed. "I wanted to solve the problem. I just had to do it at the right time. I was trying to protect you."

*Protect me.*

If he could keep choosing for me, then I didn't have to choose at all—an alibi disguised as care.

People love to package exclusion as care. My mother did it all the time—taking entire conversations she had with my father, twisting the story when whispering the details to others. *Sometimes we lie to protect the people we love.* And yet, here I was, nodding through the same trick from someone I'd agreed to marry.

When we got home, I didn't slam the car door. I didn't raise my voice. I didn't accuse him—not because I wasn't angry, but because fury was too simple for what I felt.

Instead, I unpacked the leftovers from dinner like nothing had happened.

Remmy stood in the doorway, hands shoved deep in his pockets, waiting for the next move like this might blow over if he stayed still long enough.

"You want the pasta?" I asked flatly.

He hesitated, then nodded. "Em..."

"I'm fine," I said, placing the container in the fridge with surgical precision. "You did what you thought was right."

"That's not—" He studied me, weighing whether to press or retreat. "Okay. I'll... clean up."

I tapped my foot against the kitchen floor, unsure what to do with the fury funneling through my body.

This was the second time he'd made a major decision without me. And the second time I'd caught him without even looking for it. That's what worried me—the ones I hadn't caught yet.

It started small—flowers for his mother's birthday. Before that, he'd "updated" our dinner guest list without asking. He called it helpful. He'd gone with red roses even though I'd told him she preferred tulips. He'd brushed it off as a mistake.

I remembered.

Now this.

I walked over to the edge of the counter, sliding my fingers over the cover of my wedding planner. Each page was color-coded, detailed with dates, receipts, months worth of notes. I looked up, meeting Remmy's gaze.

I picked up the planner, and dropped it into the sink. The thud was swallowed by a violent splash that seemed louder than it should have been.

Warm water sprayed, soaking both my dress and the pages, bleeding the ink into cloudy bruises. The paper swelled as if gasping, its edges curling inward. The pages drank until they buckled—petals left too long in a vase.

Ink lines fractured and spread quickly.

Remmy jumped back, eyes wide.

"I didn't mean to ruin it," he said quietly. "I thought—"

"You didn't think." My voice was cold.

He hesitated, then left.

The silence that followed was hollow, ringing in my ears. I pressed the ruined binder to my chest, the water seeping through my dress. My lists and charts were wrecked, the careful order gone.

I didn't cry. Crying was a kind of relief, and I wasn't there yet. I just felt the burn of shame creeping up my throat.

I stayed at the sink for a long time, staring at the water pooling at the bottom, clouded with swollen paper fibers. The planner was beyond saving. I pulled it out, set it on a towel, and pressed my palms to the counter until my arms shook.

This was supposed to be my control. My proof that I could keep everything in its place. Now it was limp and ruined, like it had been waiting for this moment to collapse. I wondered if that was how he saw me—like something held together just enough to serve its purpose until the first real strain came along.

The hum of the refrigerator filled the room. Outside, a car passed on the street. It all felt too normal for the way my chest was burning.

When Remmy's footsteps came down the hall again, I didn't look up. He moved slower this time, cautious. He leaned against the doorway, hands in his pockets.

"Do you want to talk about it?" he asked.

"No," I said, still wiping the counter. "I'm fine."

It was the safest lie I could offer. He left without pushing, his footsteps retreating light and unhurried, as if this was nothing more than a dinner gone wrong.

I watched the curve of his back vanish down the hall. The quiet he left behind was too clean, the kind that settles before a storm breaks. I'd grown up with that kind of quiet. It didn't comfort; it warned.

He nodded once, like he was giving me permission to keep the silence, and went upstairs again.

I stood there in the quiet, my mind spinning through every version of what tonight could have been if he'd just left things alone. Every time I landed back at the same image—Thomas standing in my reception hall, smiling like he belonged there, like he'd been invited.

I took the towel to the ruined planner, blotting at the pages without real hope. The ink smeared in gray shadows across the paper. The more I tried to save it, the worse it looked.

Something in me shifted. Not a snap, not yet. More like a quiet pivot toward something I hadn't fully admitted to myself.

That the pouch wasn't just an object in the corner of a dusty basement—it was an answer waiting for me to ask the right question. It pulsed in my mind like a secret rhythm, quiet but insistent, daring me to keep time with it.

A sharp bark from a neighbor's dog carried my attention to the kitchen window. Ms. Volkova's yard glowed faintly under her stringlights, her rows of plants standing like quiet sentinels. Even from here, I could pick out the darker blooms, the ones she never let neighborhood children get close to. My pulse quickened.

Would she be proud if I asked? Or would she narrow those sharp eyes, the way she did when pruning, and decide I wasn't ready to handle what she'd spent decades mastering?

I couldn't tell.

Some nights I imagined her handing me another bloom without hesitation, approving of my discipline, my steady hand. Other nights I imagined her pulling back, lips tight with disapproval, forcing me to stumble forward alone. She had given me the tools before. Maybe she'd give them again.

Or maybe she already knew too much.

The thought slithered through me, unsettling but magnetic. If she was watching, if she'd seen me practice, then perhaps this was always the plan: teacher and student, passing dangerous knowledge like heirlooms.

My reflection in the window looked like someone rehearsing guilt. I straightened. No—that wasn't guilt. It was anticipation, sharpened into something that made my chest ache.

I set the towel down and looked at the dark window across the fence. A single square of kitchen light blinked on, then off, like a signal I wasn't meant to catch.

Tomorrow, I would ask.

What frightened me wasn't the chance she'd refuse—it was the feeling she'd already saved me a flower.

# Chapter 10:

## Knock Knock - Who's There?

I was starting to lose my grip.

My thoughts were loud, crowding in, pacing the same short hallway until the walls bent around them.

I felt it in the way I rewrote the grocery list even though nothing was missing; how I reset the toaster dial to the same setting five times in a row.

In how I vacuumed the same rug three times in twenty minutes, or checked my phone for texts I knew weren't coming. Had I washed the knife already, or only thought about it? I touched the doorknob and couldn't tell if the metal felt warm because I'd just locked it, or because I was only imagining the click.

Sometimes I swore the rug fibers whispered against the vacuum in a different direction, as if someone else had run it before me. Maybe Matt, testing whether I'd notice.

My thinking had gone fuzzy, like I was living an inch to the left of my own body. I typically thrived on control—planned schedules, neat rows of color-coded tabs, and checkboxes ticked off with the right pen. Lately, everything blurred.

I told myself it was wedding stress. Anyone would feel off before a big day.

But that was a lie. Lies can still feel good in the mouth if you tell them often enough.

I promised myself I wouldn't poison anymore. I'd sworn it off like someone swearing off sugar, convinced I could be the rare exception who stops after one last taste. The herbology course was supposed to be my cover story, the official excuse for the stains on my fingers and the jars tucked into corners of the pantry. A hobby. A curiosity. Not evidence. Not intent.

Even sealed in the basement, the vial from Ms. Volkova had a pulse—the same woman who'd written the name I craved in bold letters—E. Byrd. I swore I could hear it beneath the refrigerator's hum, steady as a second heartbeat.

It whispered when the house was quiet, not words exactly, but an invitation. The way children hear the ice cream truck before the jingle reaches the street.

I went downstairs and retrieved it. Not to use it, just—just to feel its weight...

If Matt were standing in the doorway, he'd catalog the way my hand trembled as I lifted the vial. He'd note its exact position between the vinegar bottles, timestamp the moment I failed to keep my gaze neutral. I didn't need him present to feel cross-examined; I'd built his interrogation into my routines.

But there was no return address on the package, no trail to trace, no neat string that could lead back to my hands. That fact steadied me, a hand pressed to my shoulder in the storm.

This was safer, I lied to myself, because it wasn't rooted in Ms. Volkova's garden. Whatever stained the mug couldn't be tied to my trips to her garden—not fully.

Even when fear surged, the nearness of the plants—the way they yielded roots that smelled sharp and green, the way they thrived in a tiny glass vial—kept tugging at me.

What terrified me wasn't their danger. It was how the danger steadied me.

But tea had begun to wear the wrong costume—domestic, maternal, traceable. Matt had said the word *tea* with teeth, like something he could use later. And tea belonged to my mother. I refused to hand her the copyright to what came next.

But alcohol? Alcohol lived in this house like religion. Remmy loved the ritual more than the drink—the glass held just so, the way the bottle's neck made that hollow, rounded sound when it exhaled into crystal. Champagne promised celebration. Whiskey promised conclusion. Wine promised stories that made everyone kinder to themselves. If I wanted new theater, I needed a new prop.

I stood, restless, and drifted to the sink. The window threw my reflection back at me, doubled and faint, like a witness who wasn't sure she wanted to testify.

Outside, Ms. Volkova's yard was a dark diagram. Even at night you could feel the geometry—the order under the wild. I could almost make out the gate between our houses, the hinge she'd oiled so it never squeaked. Practical kindness. Strategic, too.

Something inside me rose from hibernation when Remmy thought he could change the vendor, to suffocate me in my carefully-orchestrated plans.

A new approach, then. Not tea. Not a kitchen ritual that smelled like lullabies. Something he would pour himself, with his own grateful hands.

I ran water over my wrists to cool the heat that anger leaves behind. In the living room, the clock only ticked when I remembered to hear it. I pictured him and Matt at the bar a few nights ago—Matt leaning back, one heel hooked against the brass rail, watching.

Not staring. Watching. That quiet cop energy without the badge: see everything, say nothing, file it alphabetically.

The mason jar waited behind the vinegar bottles, hidden but never out of mind.

All day, while I answered emails and moved through the motions of a normal life, it pulsed at the back of my awareness like a second heartbeat.

When I finally opened the pantry that evening, I felt the pull of inevitability.

The leftover powder I transferred to a mason jar labeled *Dried Herbs—Misc.*, tucked behind specialty vinegars in the cellar pantry, hidden in plain sight.

The roots were darker now, drying at their edges, their fibers curling like clenched fingers. Volkova's voice echoed in memory: *It opens doors. Gives visions. Some say glimpses of heaven, others say hell. Depends on what you carry inside yourself.*

I shaved off a sliver—barely a fingernail's worth—grinding it to dust with steady hands. The powder clung to the mortar's ridges, a ghost of what the plant had been. I muddled the roots into a paste first, working them with the pestle until they broke down to a fibrous pulp. A splash of boiling water drew out the sharp green scent, and once it cooled I strained the liquid through cheesecloth into a small jar.

The color was faint—golden, herbal—something easily mistaken for infused honey or a mixer.

I tossed anything with remnants into the sink and scrubbed it with a vigor that felt other than my own.

Ritual complete. Tools cleaned. Story prepared. It was nothing more than an herbal experiment, mixed with a blend I'd read about online but couldn't remember the source. I'd burned some of it into a skillet of honey.

Denver stationed himself in the doorway, watchful eyes fixed on me. His tilted head followed every step I took as if he understood that this wasn't just tea—it was something sharper.

"It's just tea," I whispered, though even to my own ears it sounded unconvincing.

Remmy texted five minutes before the door opened:

*Long day. Coming home. Want anything from the outside world?*

That was what he always called it—the world outside our walls. A joke. A shield.

Today, though, this sanctuary was no shield. It was my lab.

The front door shut, Denver's nails clicking across the floor in joyful welcome. Bag down, shoes off, Remmy's voice warm in greeting. The ritual of his return played out like music I'd memorized long ago.

When he stepped into the kitchen—scrubs rumpled, hair flattened by a surgical cap—his exhaustion was clear. But the moment his eyes found mine, he shifted, brightened.

As if he could change skins as easily as clothes.

"You look better," he said, leaning to kiss my cheek. "Long day?"

"Not bad. Thinking it's a margarita night," I said casually, followed by a wink.

Remmy's eyebrows raised. "Really? I'm in, but what are we celebrating?" The idea brought his hands to my waist.

"Celebrating our love." I kissed his cheek.

Remmy smiled but let his hands slip away from me. They met the back of his neck.

"Em—" he stammered. "Remember what we talked about when we first got married? When we were making a plan to succeed?"

My blood ran cold. I knew exactly what Remmy was suggesting.

When we first got engaged, Remmy suggested pre-marital therapy.

"We don't need that," I'd said, laughing like the idea was ridiculous. "People go to therapy when they're broken."

"Or before," he countered. "To stop getting broken. Prevention."

"I'd rather spend money on a trip," I insisted. "Memories, not an office."

He pressed, eager to get marriage right. "One session. If you hate it, we stop."

In the end, I agreed, because yes was cheaper than fighting. At the time, I thought I was building a future. Really, I was writing an ending.

We never visited the topic again, shifting back into our normal lives. But the incident with Thomas must have sprung the topic again, and I scrambled to find an excuse to refuse.

"I made an appointment with a professional I found," his voice was absolute. "I want to go together."

His body language suggested hope, not anger; it displayed pity, not strength. I fought to keep from rolling my eyes and sucked the air through my teeth instead.

"Okay," I said, forcing life into my voice. "We can try it."

Remmy's hands met my waist again and planted a series of pecks down my neck. "Margarita time?" he whispered in my ear.

I forced a laugh and tried to keep the rage from meeting my fingertips as I sliced the limes.

He salted the rim and I filled the cocktail glass, the gentle domestic back and forth that suggested he was back at ease.

"Cheers!" he proclaimed as he clunk his glass to mine. "To us."

I lifted my glass and winked. "To you," I said.

It truly was a celebration, but not one he was privy to. It was a celebration of innovation and change, to shifting from tea to a drink prepared together, putting the gun in his own hands.

When I poured two glasses, I only needed to dip the tip of a spoon into the jar and stir it once through his drink. The alcohol did the rest, swallowing bitterness, masking the texture.

When he finally lifted the cup, I swear the whole room inhaled with me. His lips parted. He swallowed. My chest burned as if I'd taken the sip of something scalding.

He drank as though it were nothing—just comfort at the end of a shift. He had no idea that he was already inside the experiment, that his body had been recruited as a test subject without the courtesy of consent.

The first change came forty minutes later. He rubbed his temple, eyes glassy in the lamplight. "Weird headache," he muttered, then laughed it off. "Probably dehydration. Been a while since I drank."

By fifty minutes, he shifted in his chair, hand pressing lightly to his stomach. "Feels like I might've picked up a bug. It's that season at the hospital. No more drinks for me."

I nodded, offering sympathy while memorizing the sequence:

*Headache at forty minutes. Digestive unease at fifty.*

*Fatigue, motor coordination: 55–60 minutes.*

"You okay?" I asked with just the right touch of concern.

"Yeah, just... off. Probably caught something at work." He yawned, pale now, eyes glassy.

"Maybe you should lie down," I suggested gently.

He yawned, already half-convinced. "Yeah. I'm gonna go put on the new season of *Traitors*. Thanks, Em."

Gratitude—misplaced, sincere—slipped from his lips as if I'd cared for him, not orchestrated his weakness.

I lay beside him in the dark and counted his breaths. Deeper than usual, heavy with the effort of processing what he couldn't name. He trusted me enough to surrender completely, to sleep six inches from the woman who had orchestrated his body's rebellion against itself.

Clinical notes formed in my mind with the precision of dictation:

*Headache: "Weird, it feels like someone tightened a band right here," he muttered, massaging his temples.*

*Stomach unease: "Hospital food again," he joked weakly, palm resting on his abdomen.*

*Fatigue: "Sorry, babe—can't keep my eyes open." His words slurred faintly, as if sleep tugged each syllable downward.*

I lay awake, pulse racing, and catalogued it all like data: onset, duration, intensity, resolution.

Then I heard a distinct ringing at the front door. I slid out of bed and made my way downstairs, the doorbell's echo still in my chest.

*Ding-Dong.*

I glanced at the clock: 7:43 p.m. Not an unreasonable time for a visitor, yet the sun setting outside told me this wasn't a friendly visit.

Denver's nails scratched against the hardwood as he bounded toward the door, tail wagging at the exact moment my stomach dropped. Matt's car was parked directly outside the big-picture window.

What the hell?

He'd never come unannounced. Never once used the doorbell. Typically he'd send a text or call to

Remmy, or occasionally let himself in when we'd forgotten to lock the doors.

But lately I'd been checking the locks more than once, sometimes peeling myself out of bed to check that what lay inside was safe at my hands.

When I opened the door, Matt stood on the porch—shoulders squared, jacket still on, scanning the entryway with that quiet investigator calm.

"Evening," I said, smiling just enough to sound normal. "You look like you've seen a ghost."

"Where's Remmy?" No greeting.

"Upstairs, showering," I said easily. "Hospital ran him ragged again."

Matt's gaze flicked toward the staircase. "He missed poker night."

"Oh? He mentioned maybe skipping this one." I leaned lightly on the doorframe, my tone neutral but my heartbeat steadying only because I ordered it to. "Flu season, you know. They're all short-staffed."

"Flu season," he repeated, as if testing the phrase.

I met his stare evenly. "I'll let him know you came by."

For a moment, neither of us blinked. Then he nodded once, slow, like a man filing evidence in his mind.

"Take care of him," he said.

"Always do."

I was about to shut the door gently, not slamming, not rushing—just enough control to make him wonder if he imagined my calm.

But then I heard a voice, a distinct voice. "Hi there," Ms. Volkova said. Matt turned towards her. Ms. Volkova stood, garden knife in hand, the one she used only for the thickest weeds.

My vision collapsed inside myself and tossed me into a tunnel. *Ms. Volkova's been working with Matt?*

*What did she know? What did he know?*

I felt a pain that signaled I was forcing too much strength from my teeth into the soft part of my tongue. I was about to turn and bolt inside when she spoke again—

Matt turned to me, his mouth forming spit and pausing, and for a moment I thought he was about to lean in to attack. But he dropped both arms, spit a loogie on the front patio, and turned to walk away.

Volkova's expression was unreadable, her garden knife glinting like punctuation.

"Did she welcome you in?" she asked, her tone almost polite.

Matt hesitated, then spat on the walkway and stepped back. He was gone before I could breathe.

"You should be cautious with him," Volkova said, her gaze never leaving mine. "Men who notice too much rarely survive it."

It took everything in me to hold the weight of my spine as she stared at me, her lips pursed in an expression I'd never seen. Her eyes were a different color—darker, all crystal lost—something I couldn't quite attribute to the darkness.

Ms. Volkova's words drowned my ears: *You should be cautious with him. Men who notice too much rarely survive it.*

She didn't respond when I muttered "Thank you" under my breath; when I turned back into the threshold that marked my life safe.

I closed the door, peering at her through the peephole, deathly curious.

Those pursed lips held at my door, when suddenly she started towards the porch. My body tensed as she walked up the steps, then her feet stood inches from me—the weight of wood holding us apart.

But suddenly she bent out of sight, disappearing. I ran upstairs as fast as I could while keeping my feet mute on the carpetless steps. By the time I approached the bedroom window that oversaw the door, I saw her hovering over the circle where Matt had left his saliva, sticking a Q-Tip into a tiny test-tube.

Then she stood, wiping her dress—knife still in hand—and headed down the steps, disappearing into the dark.

My hands trembled as I slipped under the covers, forcing my eyes shut, listening to the quiet roar that signaled Remmy was asleep.

The house had gone still again. Denver curled at the foot of the bed, chest rising and falling with the kind of steady rhythm that belonged only to creatures without conscience. Beside me, Remmy remained on his back, one arm flung over his head, the soft rise of his stomach marked by breaths he would never think to guard.

Once, nights like this had felt electric. I'd lie here in the dark, my own pulse racing, memorizing every shift of his chest, every twitch of his fingers, every sigh that might reveal the substance working its way through him. It had been thrilling—scientific. The meticulous cataloguing of onset, escalation, resolution.

I had filled notebooks with numbers, columns, and sketches of symptoms like a child tracing butterflies into jars. But tonight, there was nothing to write.

I didn't reach for my pen. I didn't need to. The experiments had already taught me everything they could. Three trials was plenty, four a risky test, like touching the stove when you already know it's hot. The thrill had curdled into something else—something heavier, simpler.

I no longer cared about variables or precision. I no longer wanted charts and data that explained his body's rebellion.

I wanted to be the woman others see on the other side of the wedding.

It was too close now. Too many near-misses. Matt's eyes narrowing in doorways, his voice shaping questions without asking them outright. Volkova's flowers exchanged like secrets I could never return. Every close call was a thread pulling at the hem of my disguise, and I felt the whole garment straining.

I turned onto my side, studying the line of Remmy's profile lit faintly by the alarm clock's glow. He looked young in sleep, untroubled. It made me think of my father before the sickness, before the tea. That same trusting slackness in the mouth. That same belief that a closed door meant safety.

My fingers itched, not for a pen, not for the legal pad waiting downstairs, but for the final vial. The one still hidden, waiting like a promise.

The trial phase was over. This was the conclusion— the part where results get published, where the story ends.

I laid my hand lightly against his chest, feeling the steady pump of his heart beneath skin and bone. In a matter of days, this same thrum would be silenced. By my hand. By my will.

And when it stopped, so would the questions. No more experiments, no more risks. Only one clean ending.

I smiled into the pillow. I could already hear the word they would use: *widow.* The doctor's wife who lost him too soon. The tragic young bride left standing in white beside an empty space.

For the first time in weeks, I felt at peace.

But peace was fragile.

Matt's face at the door lingered behind my eyelids longer than Remmy's did.

Until I wondered if maybe I'd been testing the wrong subject all along.

# Chapter 11:

# Therapy

I woke to sunlight spilling across the curtains, warm and heavy, like the house had decided to grant me a reprieve. Denver was curled in his usual crescent at the foot of the bed, sighing into his paws, and Remmy was still sleeping beside me, his mouth just barely parted.

For the first time in weeks, I felt a strange kind of triumph in my bones.

I'd handled it. Handled *him*.

I'd outlasted the night—Matt's suspicion, Volkova's warning—and the quiet felt like permission.

I rolled onto my back, savoring the calm. The ledger of trials and doses, the midnight notes, the careful disguises—all of it seemed to fade under the realization that I had proven myself. I had survived the scrutiny. Even under Matt's hawk gaze, I hadn't cracked.

Remmy stirred beside me, rubbing his eyes. His voice came rough, low. "Morning." He kissed my shoulder, soft, habitual. "Headache's still hanging on. Weird, right? Usually gone by now."

The words caught me—not because the headache mattered, but because it lingered. For the first time, something had carried into the morning. My heart thudded once, hard. Then I smoothed my face into sympathy. "Probably just stress. You've been running on fumes."

He nodded but then pushed up on his elbows, suddenly alert. "Hey, remember? The therapist I found had a cancellation. She called yesterday. She can see us today."

The word *therapist* slid under my skin like a blade.

I smiled anyway, because "no" had already been stripped from my vocabulary weeks ago. "That's great," I said, my voice bright enough to be believed.

"Yeah," he said, relief in his grin. "It's perfect timing, right before the wedding. Like a tune-up."

I leaned back into the pillows, letting him talk, letting the plans form in his mouth instead of mine. But inside, my mind sharpened against the sudden shift. A session meant exposure. Another pair of eyes. Another witness.

Still, I had no reason to refuse. Not without raising questions I couldn't afford.

As he padded into the bathroom, humming, I pressed my palm flat against the quilt. The headache, the therapist, Volkova's gaze—all of it wrapped tight around my chest.

But pride still pulsed beneath it. Matt hadn't won. Not yet.

And as long as Remmy believed I was trying, no one would suspect what I was saving for the end.

I replayed the moment in my head like a short VCR jammed on repeat—the look in Matt's eyes as he finally released his hands from beside me, the small defeat carved into his face.

That thought followed me through the motions: while I made Remmy breakfast, while I brushed my teeth, while I started the car. It hummed in the background even when Remmy touched my leg and pointed out license plates on the road, filling the silence with his easy chatter.

I carried it with me as I sat down beside him in the waiting room.

The therapist's office had four rainbows on the wall, a neutral cardigan, and a neutral voice. She smiled with professional warmth. "What brings you here?"

"Nothing. Well, something," Remmy said quickly, then laughed. "Sorry—never done therapy before."

"It's okay." She was soft with Remmy, reassuring him with a nod. The fluorescent lights grew louder.

"See, I procrastinate and tell myself it's because I want to help Emily. The problem is that I'm realizing it's actually me acting selfishly, wanting to avoid the problem."

"Could you say what you're thinking more directly?" A tiny nod of encouragement.

"I want to be better. To be the perfect partner for Emily." He scooted closer and squeezed my hand.

She put her hand to her heart; I grit my teeth.

"What is it that you want to improve?" She started making light notes onto a sketchpad.

Remmy sat up straighter. "I want to learn to appreciate what she does for me, to never second guess her motives."

The word *motives* sat like a thorn in my side, instant.

The therapist's eyes glinted with an emotion I couldn't place, and she stopped writing. She leaned forward in her seat. I could feel the heat of my chest turning red.

"What are you second guessing?" She looked at Remmy carefully, encouraging. Her eyes were soft and invited more.

Remmy looked at me as if for permission, but his eyes quickly shifted back to hers. "I love Emily, but sometimes..." He paused, glazing out the window. "Sometimes I feel like the people around me don't understand her, make grand assumptions that make me second-guess."

The words stung the air, and Remmy's eyes held the glass. The therapist nodded, letting his words hold weight for a moment.

She turned to me.

"What about you, Emily? What brings you here today?"

"I'm sure I have room to grow," I said smoothly.

She tilted her head, pressing back. "Can you share a little more about that?"

I fought the urge to roll my eyes. I could play her game. "My anger. I can be angry, but nothing more than the next person."

She smiled, though her smile mimicked mine when I practiced in the mirror.

"What do you think about what Remmy had to say?" Her head remained tilted. My fingers picked the frays of my jeans.

I wanted to say *it's none of his business, nor is it yours.* Matt's name was more consistent in my mind, in my mouth than I'd ever signed up for.

I wanted to turn to Remmy, ask him what he'd known—what Matt planted in his mind and whether he believed it.

Instead, I chose an out. "I think Remmy is very sweet, but sometimes, he can be very impressionable." I peeked at Remmy whose gaze was still fixed outside.

I continued without prompting. "His friends—well, friend—has become a big part of our lives. He's around constantly, always suggesting I'm up to no good." My temples pulsed and the words slipped out before I could consider the consequences. "I'd like Remmy and I to be just that—Remmy and *I*." I felt the word "I" vibrate through the room, more forceful than intended.

The air hung between us. I tried to steady my pulse. Remmy stared outside.

The therapist leaned back, studying me. "What do you love about Remmy?"

The question caught me off guard. "His kindness," I said quickly, then forced a smile. "He has a gentle heart. Reliable, loyal. I understand him."

Her pen paused, eyes narrowing just slightly before turning to Remmy. "And you? What do you love about Emily?"

Remmy turned from the window for the first time and placed his arm around the small of my back behind the couch.

"She takes care of me in little ways. When my favorite team was in the World Cup, Emily made custom shirts, just for us. She even made cookies with little soccer balls on them." Remmy's foot was bouncing, excitement in his voice. "Always making dinner, tea... Like once, I had a stomach bug and she made ginger tea—so thoughtful. Too bad I actually got sicker. But you see she's always trying to help." He looked at me, laughing softly at an inside joke I desperately wanted to be separated from.

The therapist's pen paused. Just a fraction, but I saw it. Her eyes flicked to me, calm but sharper.

"What kind of tea?" she asked.

"Ginger, with honey. I think." Remmy smiled sheepishly. "I love when Emily gives. Sometimes I wish she asked if I was ready to receive."

The pen moved again. That deliberate silence therapists weaponize. Then her gaze cut to me.

"I like making tea," I said evenly. "It soothes me too. I probably brewed it too strong."

She smiled—thin, professional—but minutes later she circled back. "Tell me more about the tea. How does it feel, Remmy, being cared for that way?"

"It feels... good. But sometimes I feel expected to be grateful for things I didn't really want. That's on me, though. I need to learn to receive."

Her pen scratched. Her gaze lingered. I kept my face soft, my smile practiced. "He hates letting people do nice things. Even Christmas gifts."

Remmy laughed, embarrassed. The tension broke—but I felt her eyes again.

She'd marked me.

Throughout the remainder of the session, I found myself staring at the clock, like the hand would move faster if I watched it. We were rounding the end of the session, and it was time to wrap-up.

"When will I see you for another session? I typically ask new couples to come consecutively for four weeks, so I can get a fair assessment." She looked between Remmy and I, holding my eye contact on *fair assessment.*

Before Remmy could answer, I cut in. "We'll need to discuss it. Something we'll discuss as a team. A partnership." I smiled.

Remmy shrugged and stood, thanking her for her time. He chatted the entire way to the car.

I turned back to the building and caught her, staring through the slant of her blinds. The laptop glow in her glasses. Still watching.

That night, Remmy cooked pasta. Over-salted, but proud. He asked what I thought of therapy.

"It was fine," I said. "But we don't need it."

"You sure? I liked it. Felt like a reset."

"We don't need a reset."

He nodded, obedient, though not convinced.

Matt's voice lingered, even when he wasn't in the room.

He knew. Or maybe he didn't. Maybe he was only circling. Maybe I was the one building shapes out of smoke.

But then the therapist. Her pen scratching, her gaze slicing through me with that soft professional smile that was anything but soft. I could still hear the way she said it: *Tell me more about the tea.* Innocent words, but weighted, like she'd chosen them knowing they'd land sharp.

A neutral cardigan and neutral smile that hadn't been neutral at all.

I saw her blinds every time I closed my eyes—tilted just enough for her to watch, to take notes on me long after the session ended.

Fog edged into my vision as I rested on the couch, though my mind was anything but calm. The ceiling warped, the shadows shifted like they wanted to lean closer. I thought of my mother—her mug of bitter liquid, her voice whispering praise in my ear. I thought of Volkova, her mud-stained gloves handing me roots without a single question, as if she already knew what I'd do.

The wedding was no longer a distant date on a calendar. It was here—its weight threaded into every ribbon tied, every program folded, every smile rehearsed in the mirror.

Even under the scrutiny, for the first time in weeks, I felt still. Matt hadn't undone me. The therapist hadn't pierced me. Even Remmy's soft persistence couldn't shake the knowledge that the end was mine to write.

Control sat in my chest like a steady drumbeat. I'd survived the rehearsals, the trials, the careful concealments. I'd walked the tightrope and hadn't fallen. And now—just days from the vows—I wasn't looking for symptoms anymore. I wasn't interested in timelines or variables. I wanted the conclusion.

That meant one more step.

I glanced out the kitchen window toward Volkova's yard, the geometry of her garden sharp even in the morning haze. My fingers rested on the counter, tapping out an unspoken rhythm.

A vial of poision sat a floor away in the basement yet I couldn't shake the feeling that I needed the final step to come from *her* garden.

I'd need to see her. Not for instruction, not for education, not even for reassurance. This time, I needed something permanent.

One final flower.

But I was on thin ice. The incident with Matt at my door—his spit glistening on my stone walkway—

hadn't done me any favors in my relationship with Ms. Volkova. She'd rescued me from my last dosing, her disapproval sharp as a ruler smacked across the knuckles.

This wasn't for more trials. I didn't want notes, dosages, symptoms anymore.

Volkova was on the guest list—her RSVP already marked *Attending*. She knew the ceremony was nearly here. She would recognize the shape of this request, the inevitability behind it.

What I wasn't sure of was how much of my plan she already understood. And to get my hands on what I wanted, I'd have to hint at it—just enough to make her complicit, without ever saying the word.

But the silence pressed the moment into a brick in my stomach. My own mind whispered treachery: *It's time.*

On the wedding night itself—when trust was at its highest, when no one would suspect—I would need something final. A bloom that didn't teach or mimic illness, but finished.

Volkova had it. I was sure she did. And I would take it, because there was something electric I couldn't name when I thought about the final dosage stemming from her yard.

She was in her garden again, as if she'd never left it. Always tending, pruning, pulling—like the dirt itself needed her constant presence to stay alive. Her gloves were streaked with a darker stain today, something that looked less like soil and more like bruises smeared across the canvas.

The smell emitting from her garden was different in the cool of the morning, where the water from the lake still hovered in the air, mixing with dirt. Sweet, heavy, narcotic—the kind of fragrance that didn't belong in a suburban yard but in some tropical dream.

The air clung to my skin, damp with dawn, and every step toward Volkova's fence.

"I wanted to thank you... for last night." My throat was tight.

She didn't move, didn't acknowledge the desperate woman standing in front of her.

I circled my thumb on the sharp of the fence.

"But I think I need... more."

"I knew the first day you moved in," she said softly, still facing the dirt. "Some people tend to nurture, others prune. You? You were always meant to prune."

The words hung there—neither approval nor warning—just recognition.

Only then did she straighten, eyes narrowing against the sun. For the first time, hesitation flickered there. Not disapproval, not surprise—hesitation.

"Your wedding is still days away, no?" Her tone was mild, but she kept her back to me, picking at her gloves. "Why would you need another now?"

I shifted, trying not to act like I didn't suddenly feel unclothed. "This is the last time I'll ask." I could barely choke out the words.

She turned and studied me in silence, the pause stretching long enough that I thought she might actually say no. My pulse thudded at the thought. The deeper she stared, I couldn't tell if paranoia was capturing me or if her eyes had truly turned the color of rain.

If she refused, I wasn't sure what I would do— whether I'd risk improvisation, or whether the entire plan would unravel.

"I want to learn more about the flowers, maybe one day become an expert... like you," I added, keeping my back strong like hers.

Volkova finally raised her eyes, scanning me in a way that felt less like assessment and more like confirmation. "Of course you do."

Finally, she sighed, set down her shears, and moved toward the shaded side of the garden where the more dangerous plants were kept. She worked the soil with gloved hands, drawing out a bloom that hung like lanterns, long trumpets of pale gold and cream, their edges flaring delicately, their weight dragging them earthward. They looked like instruments held upside down, waiting for some invisible musician to draw sound from them.

Roots dangled like nerves. She brushed away excess dirt, then dangled it over the fence.

"Brugmansia," Volkova said softly, almost reverently. "Most people call them Angel's Trumpets. Beautiful, aren't they?"

The beauty was undeniable, but it was the wrong kind of beauty—the kind that asked you to come closer even as every instinct whispered that closeness was dangerous.

The bloom sat in her hand, impossible in its perfection. The petals curled outward like beckoning fingers, their edges trembling as though they breathed. Shades of violet bled into indigo, then into the faintest trace of silver, each fold alive with light that shifted when she tilted her palm.

It was a beauty that felt intentional, deliberate— like the flower knew it was being admired and reveled in it. Every curve seemed to invite her closer, every shimmer a whispered promise. For a moment I couldn't imagine beauty existing outside of it; the whole world felt pale beside that bloom.

"Dangerous," she warned.

The bloom sat in her hand, radiating heat like a living sun. Its petals seemed to breathe, pulsing upward in waves that defied gravity.

I reached out to accept its offerings, but she snapped it back, her fist tightening around the bloom like a secret she wasn't ready to release.

"Not yet," she said, voice steady, as though nothing had shifted. She set the bundle at her feet with deliberate care and bent once more toward her garden. My pulse was still caught in the silence she'd left behind, but her hands moved with practiced calm, tugging weeds from the soil, neat and methodical, as if the air hadn't just thickened into something that could choke me.

She returned to her rhythm seamlessly, her back to me, her movements ordinary—too ordinary—like the moment had never happened at all.

"Come back when you're ready to use it," she said into the dirt. "Limits accidents."

My neck flushed red.

She didn't trust me, not until it was time.

The incident with Matt in the doorframe changed the dynamic of trust between a mentor and mentee; gardener and observer; neighbor and friend.

I turned and made for the house, steps clumsy and exposed, like a college student in the humiliating glare of a walk of shame.

I'd barely set my foot on the first step when she called out, her voice carrying over the fence like a command.

"Weeds come back faster than you think. Especially the ones that walk and talk." Her voice came out flat and certain.

"Matt." The name slipped like a thorn under my tongue.

She gave the smallest shrug as if she'd somehow heard me. "That boy comes around often. Always the same jacket, with a button missing on the left cuff. You've noticed?"

I hadn't, but the specificity told me she had.

"He's a weed that grows fast," she went on. "And weeds spread faster when you cut them the wrong way."

I nodded, letting the words hang between us. I found myself drawn to the closet upstairs.

The sleeves were perfect. The lace looked delicate, petal-like, as if stitched from the same veins that carried poison through Volkova's flowers. They looked like they'd been part of the original design, integrated so seamlessly that no one would guess they'd been added by someone who understood the difference between decoration and disguise.

*Beautiful things require patience*, Ms. Volkova had written, *Some gardens require blood to bloom properly.*

And she was right. I'd been patient for months, learning and preparing and waiting for the right moment to transform theoretical knowledge into decisive action.

I sat on the carpet of the closet and picked at loose strings.

They were all circling now—Matt, the therapist's watchful eyes, even Volkova with her denial.

And Remmy—sweet, oblivious Remmy—talking about sleep like it was a gift I'd given him, not a symptom. His trust was a wound he didn't know he had.

Every "thank you," every kiss, every sigh of relief when his headache faded made me feel the air tightening around me. Because what if he noticed more than he let on? What if his gratitude was really caution?

I caught myself glancing at him too often, tracing the vein at his wrist, watching the pulse tick like a metronome counting down my time.

Remmy walked back in a few hours later, wrapping his arms around me from behind while I stood at the counter, pressing his face into the curve of my neck.

"What's this?" he asked, nodding toward the bowl in front of me.

"Dinner," I said. "You're spoiled, remember?"

Spoiling someone is just controlled generosity, though. I liked what I could measure.

Control was easier in the kitchen. I could decide when the water boiled, how much heat touched the pan, when to take something off before it burned. People weren't like that—too many hidden burners, too many ways to scorch when you weren't looking.

He chuckled, pressing another joke between us. "Chef Em."

We moved around each other in the kitchen with practiced ease—two people who'd learned the choreography of sharing space without stepping on toes.

He took out the trash. I set the table. We passed, brushed, sidestepped like it was muscle memory.

My mind was fixed on the root dangling from Ms. Volkova's wrist.

At dinner, he told me about the bar. Matt had gotten into it with a guy over some nonsense sports stat.

Remmy always told stories in the same arc: a harmless beginning, a little tension in the middle, an easy laugh to tie it off. But tonight, the edges frayed. He took longer to find words, left pauses hanging just long enough for me to notice, then smoothed them over with that practiced grin.

There was a tequila shot that "shouldn't have happened," followed by a karaoke dare that became a twenty-minute debate about 90s boy bands.

He mimicked the off-key chorus, half-singing, half-laughing, and I pictured the scene: sticky bar tops, neon lights buzzing, strangers egging him on. I could almost hear the laughter, feel the secondhand embarrassment.

But beneath it, his eyes flicked away like even the memory of the song cost him more energy than it should.

It all sounded harmless. Almost charming. But I watched the flush in his cheeks, the way he kept reaching for his water like he couldn't quite quench something.

"I love this," he said, pointing his fork at the chicken. "It's... buttery? But not greasy?"

"Lemon," I said. "It balances things."

He smiled at me. "You balance things."

I counted his bites. Counted again. Numbers were safe. They didn't care about guilt or intention. There was no threat in his food, but I was addicted to studying his patterns.

Researchers wanted patterns. I wasn't interested in chaos—I wanted a result I could point to, like a solved equation no one else had the patience to work through.

Like Ms. Volkova in her garden—clipping, watering, waiting.

"So," he said carefully, "about the DJ thing..."

"I know I didn't handle it well," he went on. "I should've told you before I made the switch. I just didn't want to pile more on your plate—between the budget stress, your mom stuff..."

I kept my voice even. "I'm not mad."

That caught him off guard. "Really?"

"I get it. You wanted to do it your way. I was controlling. You made a call. It's done."

He studied me like he wasn't sure if this was a trap. "I expected a speech. Or a spreadsheet."

I danced my fork around my plate. "You're off the hook this time."

His shoulders eased. "Thanks, Em. I mean it. You've been amazing lately."

I nodded, turning back to the stove. "Just want the day to go well."

What I didn't say, what I barely admitted to myself, was that my attention had shifted. I used to obsess over centerpieces, playlists, table placements. Now those details felt like set dressing.

The real story would happen after the last song. Everything else was noise. The centerpieces, the playlists—they were only there to frame the final, deliberate moment.

Right then, Remmy got a phone call from a number he didn't recognize, sending it to voicemail. But twenty minutes later when the dishes were clean and I left to do laundry, Remmy appeared, phone in hand.

"So weird—the therapist just called me. Said she wanted to meet with me alone."

A blanket of heat wrapped around my body. "What?"

"Yeah," he continued, clearly confused. "She said she wanted to ask some follow up questions, asked if I'm still drinking tea that made me sick."

The air thinned. It wasn't strange. It was dangerous. Someone had looked at me, studied me, and then called him privately. That wasn't outreach—it was surveillance. It was exposure.

I wanted to snatch the phone from his hands, to dial the number and tell her she knows nothing. But I continued tending to the laundry, acting as natural as I could with hands that suddenly felt foreign.

My pulse spiked. Another trap door opening beneath my feet. I heard my voice before I could think it through, sharp and certain:

"Rem, she's into you." The words came out of my mouth before I could process them. "It happens all the time, classic story—it was totally obvious."

He blinked. "What? No—she didn't sound—"

"Don't be naive." The words cracked like a whip. "Inviting you alone? After seeing us together? That's not professional. She wanted an excuse."

"But she—"

I set down the towel I was folding, turning to him. "Rem, she practically talked to you the entire time. I was like, 'hello, I'm here too.' I'd appreciate it if you ignored her. We'll find a man next time."

He hesitated, confusion lingering like smoke. Doubt. I saw it flicker across his face, the dangerous kind that suggested a thought he'd never spoken: *What if Emily is the problem?*

For a terrifying moment, I thought I'd lost him. The silence stretched too long. I could feel the entire house listening.

Then something shifted. His jaw set. Protectiveness snapped back into place. He needed to believe me more than he needed to question me.

"You're probably right," he said slowly, testing the words as though they might crumble in his mouth. "It just felt... off."

"Exactly." I cupped his face, pressing my thumb against the ridge of his cheekbone like I was stamping him with certainty. "We're fine."

He softened, the lines of his face loosening. Relief seeped in—relief that I was steering again, that he didn't have to doubt what I'd just made clear for him. It was enough to send him retreating toward the garage to work on his project car, his version of stress management.

But my hands shook as I wiped down the counter.

Hollow things echo—and echoes always come back.

# Chapter 12:

## This Is It

Two days. The house felt crowded with eyes even when it was empty.

Matt's too-long glances. The therapist's too-precise questions. Even Remmy's casual comments, the way he mentioned tea like it was an innocent anecdote—every word replayed in my head like evidence presented at trial.

There were no more experiments, no more tea, no more doses, no more risks. The ledger had to stay closed if I wanted to survive the next seventy-two hours.

But paranoia didn't obey rules. It seeped under doors and into my bloodstream.

When Matt texted a meme—nothing suspicious, nothing more than brotherly teasing—I caught myself staring at it for ten minutes, wondering if it was code. *Did he know? Was he warning me?*

When Remmy kissed me goodnight, his lips soft against mine, I wondered if he could taste the chemicals lingering against my skin.

It made sense now—Matt had been the one to recommend her. His therapist, his safety net. No wonder her questions about the tea had landed like rehearsed lines from his script.

Her voicemail had come to him—never to us—like she already knew which mouth would answer.

When I looked in the mirror, I wondered if my mother's face was finally breaking through mine.

She used to test everything—me, neighbors, even the garden. Once she left my goldfish unfed for a week "to see if it would fight to live." When it died, she said the weak didn't deserve to stay.

Control was her religion; mercy was just another word for laziness.

I'd learned early on that love was something you proved by surviving it. Maybe that's why every experiment now felt like devotion, not destruction.

I sat at the kitchen table with my planner open, pen uncapped, and no words to write. The page warped where water had once soaked it, curling in on itself, like even paper knew it was dangerous to hold my secrets.

Denver snored at my feet, his trust steady and unbroken. The only creature in this house who hadn't noticed the change in me.

Two days. That was all I had to survive. Two days of silence. Two days of pretending to be harmless.

But even as I told myself that, my eyes kept flicking to the pantry. To the shelf where the mason jar sat hidden, its roots pressed against glass, patient and waiting.

Like me.

A week earlier, Matt had dropped by unannounced, standing in the doorway while I stirred tea for Remmy. I hadn't seen him at first. The jar's lid was already in my hand when I turned, smiling too fast.

"Just honey powder," I'd said, shaking a pinch into the mug, my voice light. His eyes had tracked the motion, then the jar, then me.

He'd nodded, too casually—but something had already changed in the way he looked at me after that.

My suitcase lay open on the bedroom floor, half-packed. I'd been adding items systematically—clothes for the various pre-wedding events, shoes that had been broken in sufficiently to wear for extended periods, jewelry that would complement the dress without competing for attention.

And carefully hidden among the ordinary necessities of bridal preparation, I'd placed my other supplies.

Everything required for the practical application of months of theoretical research, camouflaged among the legitimate tools that women used to make themselves beautiful for important occasions.

I'd also packed a sachet of valerian root purchased from the health food store—harmless material that looked similar enough to more dangerous preparations that it could serve as evidence of innocent intent if anyone ever needed to search my belongings.

An insurance policy that would support the narrative of a bride who'd been experimenting with natural sleep aids for wedding stress rather than someone who'd been planning murder with botanical precision.

When I walked down the aisle, I would carry two bouquets—the one people saw, and the one I had already hidden away.

After the ceremony, they would find valerian among my things. Harmless valerian for anxiety and insomnia, perfectly reasonable for someone dealing with the pressure of organizing a major social event. No one would think to test what had actually been administered, especially if the death appeared to be from natural causes that fit his family's medical history.

The perfect crime wasn't complicated—it was simple, obvious, hiding in plain sight among explanations that people wanted to believe rather than alternatives that required them to confront uncomfortable truths about human nature.

I sealed the cosmetics bag and placed it in the interior pocket of my suitcase, where it would be protected from casual observation but accessible when the time came for practical application.

The dress hung on my closet door, sleeves catching the afternoon light that filtered through our bedroom windows. *Beautiful things require patience*, Ms. Volkova had written, and she was right. I'd been patient for months, learning and preparing and waiting for the right moment to transform theoretical knowledge into decisive action.

That patience was almost over. Soon, I would not just be a bride. I would be the plant in full bloom—roots hidden, petals open, beautiful enough to distract from the poison waiting underneath.

The wedding would be the culmination of everything I'd studied, the practical examination that would demonstrate whether I'd truly mastered the subject matter or had only succeeded in convincing myself that I understood principles I couldn't actually apply.

I wasn't walking toward a husband. I was walking toward immortality. Toward the end of ever being ordinary.

In days, I would walk down the aisle toward a man who trusted me completely, who had no idea that his bride was carrying death in her cosmetics bag along with lipstick and mascara and all the other tools women used to make themselves beautiful for the cameras that would document their happiness.

Remmy tapped the sketchpad still lying on the counter. "After the honeymoon, I'll start building that table. We'll eat a hundred dinners at it, just us." He kissed me once and left the room.

Upstairs, my crawlspace notebook sat zipped into my cosmetics bag—*Foxglove, Wolfsbane, Oleander*—each entry underlined like scripture. His sketches dreamed of permanence. Mine promised it, but only in silence.

I glanced at the pad, his lines, his dreams. Then I closed it softly. His table would never hold a single meal.

The thought should have terrified me. Instead, it felt like graduation: the bloom after months of careful cultivation, petals wide, roots deep, ready to prove whether I had truly mastered what I'd been growing toward all along.

I was ready. The dress was ready. The materials were ready.

All that remained was patience for a few more days, followed by the kind of decisive action that separated people who fantasized about power from people who actually wielded it when circumstances demanded results.

***

The day before the wedding on the way to the venue, I couldn't stop glancing in the rearview mirror at the dress hanging in the back seat, knowing Ms. Volkova had added her touch. It loomed like a passenger, silk swaying each time I hit a bump.

"This is gorgeous, Rem!" Marlene called from across the parking lot before we were even out of the car. She folded him into a hug, her movements swift and practiced, like she'd been rehearsing.

The air smelled of hot asphalt, sharp enough to sting.

Here was Remmy, edges rounded by his family's warmth. And me, sharpened by mine. We were playing opposite games—his built for comfort, mine for survival.

Marlene squint-smiled and wrapped me in a hug that smelled of essential oils and sunscreen. "We're so glad to see you doing well," she said, pulling back. "Remmy told us you've been stressed—we weren't sure which version of you we'd get today. Seeing you smiling means the world."

I blinked. Smiled. Swallowed. "Doing my best."

We unloaded the trunk: garment bags, boxes of favors, the rolling suitcase with the squeaky wheel. Remmy morphed into cruise director, eager to carry everything at once. Chuck picked up a bag labeled "groomsmen gifts" as if unsure whether it was fragile or sacred.

Inside, the venue transformed us. Stone walls and chandeliers, air tinged with polished wood and pine needles. The kind of place where cold lingered in corners, a castle pretending to be warm. Even my footsteps felt reluctant, like the stone was waiting to take something in exchange for passage.

"It's like a storybook," Marlene cooed. "Didn't you say this used to be a convent?"

Remmy grinned. "Yeah. Emily found it. Total gem, right?"

He turned to me, beaming like a kid unveiling a science project. "Hey—it's really happening, huh?"

He kissed my temple, hand resting at the small of my back. It should have grounded me. Instead, I felt tethered—anchored by him, but with scissors already hidden in my other hand.

"Yeah," I murmured. "We're doing it."

At the front desk, the concierge checked us in with that bright, rehearsed politeness. Room keys, a map, reminders about breakfast hours.

The building was compact—two floors, just enough rooms to hold the wedding party without chaos. Extended family would scatter to cabins down the road. Local guests would slip away after dessert, driving home under a sky thick with stars.

Two elevators anchored the building, each opening onto hushed landings with thick carpets and black-and-white photos of the property's history—nuns in habit, stone archways under snow. Pictures that pressed your voice lower without asking.

Remmy hooked my pinky with his and swung our hands like children.

I glanced sideways at him. His face was open. Happy. Content.

But mine was focused.

At the rehearsal dinner, Matt caught me by the elbow when no one was watching. His grip was steady, not cruel, but unyielding. "If something happens to him," he whispered, "I'll know it was you." Then he released me with a smile, as if he'd only complimented my dress.

His warning didn't shake me—it clarified the next step. The flower would solve both problems at once.

I told Remmy I wanted time away to prepare, yet I yearned to get my hands on the gift Ms. Volkova had promised.

Remmy didn't question it, only offering to join. I rejected, urging him to get a head start on sleep.

For the first time, I didn't find the silhouette of Ms. Volkova in her garden when she expected me. I stood on my back porch, keys in hand, and tugged at the sleeve of my shirt.

I'd never approached her doorstep, never felt the shape of her doorbell or weight of her door knocker. Never really took time to examine her front yard, now that I'd considered it.

I found myself standing in front of her steps with a whisper that told me to turn around. But behind the wooden doors stood the one woman who held what I needed more than anything.

My pulse matched my knock. Minutes passed before I heard the lock click open.

"You've come," she said, voice even. Not a question.

I half-expected her to laugh, to dismiss me, to ask what I thought I was doing. Instead, she studied me the way she studied her plants—quietly, as though she was deciding if I could survive harsher weather.

But right as I motioned to turn away, she produced a plant from somewhere unseen. One second her hands were empty, the next she was holding it out between us, like an offering or a challenge.

What she revealed bloomed pale and heavy, pendulous blossoms shaped like trumpets hanging down in silence. Their color was impossible to pin down—white at first, but with a shimmer at the edges that caught the light.

Leaves darker, petals heavier, stems thick as wrists. It looked like it stemmed from another universe.

The stem trembled slightly in the air, petals angled toward me like a warning flare. It wasn't just a flower—it was a verdict, a silent sentence. She might as well have handed me a vial marked with a black cross, the kind you'd find sketched in the margins of an old apothecary's ledger to signal poison.

For a beat, neither of us spoke. The weight of it existed entirely in the space between her hand and mine. I couldn't tell if she was giving me permission or testing whether I'd reach.

When I did, my fingers brushed the leaves, and I felt a jolt—cold recognition, like touching a relic you've only ever read about. The plant was alive, but it pulsed with something closer to finality than growth.

Her eyes flicked to mine. Not approval, not warning. Something in between.

"Beautiful. Deceptive. Everything about it is poison—leaves, seeds, flowers. Even the scent, if you linger too long."

The blossoms swayed slightly in the air, though there was no wind. My nervous system was fully activated; I could taste my teeth.

"I trust you to be safe with it," she continued, her voice calm as if reciting a recipe. "This flower is beautiful." She paused, trapping me with her stare. "It stops the heart."

I couldn't speak.

She let me look at it, as though she wanted me to understand that this was not an herb, not a root, not a simple experiment. This was a threshold.

"Do you want it?" she asked.

My mouth was dry. My pulse pounded so hard I could hear it. I thought of the therapist's eyes, of Matt's careful questions, of Remmy's trusting breath in the dark. My vision narrowed.

"Yes."

Her hand moved with no hesitation. She lessened her grip on the bloom and placed it in mine, lingering a second longer than necessary. The weight of it surprised me—light in appearance, yet heavy, too heavy, as if it carried its own gravity.

Volkova didn't lecture, didn't warn again. She only said: "Keep it sealed until you're certain. This one doesn't forgive mistakes."

Her voice dropped to a whisper I could barely hear. "This is not a trial flower. This is not for experiments. If I hand it to you, there is no more tending after. Do you understand?"

I nodded, the beat of my heart keeping time with the air's silence.

"Careful, Emily. Some gardens you can replant. Others you salt forever."

"I don't bless this," she said at last, "I only acknowledge it."

I swallowed, feeling the bloom's weight in my palm like an oath. "Forever's what I'm asking for."

She didn't speak. The wind picked up, giving sound to the silence between us.

Finally, she nodded and turned back inside.

The bundle sat on my kitchen table like a gift too exquisite to open, laid in yesterday's newspaper. The paper was tucked neatly around the stem as if modesty could conceal what it really was. After I finished the remainder of tasks I'd come back for—like grabbing the exit bubbles I'd forgotten—I unfolded it carefully, the way one would unwrap a relic, not a plant—hands steady, breath shallow.

The bloom was extraordinary, almost indecent in its perfection. Petals layered like silk veils, white blushing into pale violet, edges tinged faintly with a darker hue as if someone had painted warning lines into its design. The veins pulsed faintly in the light, a network delicate enough to invite admiration and sinister enough to remind me what I held.

This was not just a flower. This was a sentence, a curtain drop, the last line in a story I'd been rehearsing for months. Its beauty felt purposeful, like nature's way of disguising how much power lived in the fibers below. I traced the stem with my fingertip, then turned it to study the roots—the true treasure.

Widowhood shimmered in my mind like an image half-formed: me in black, shoulders squared, tears timed to the cameras. The tragic young bride with her life cracked open before it began. People would whisper words like *fate* and *cruelty*, no one would whisper *choice*. That knowledge lived only here, in my kitchen, in this flower.

With deliberate patience, I set the bloom aside and laid the roots on the cutting board. They were thick, knotted, the color of damp earth. I ground them slowly in the mortar, every turn of the pestle steady and clean. The fibers resisted at first, then gave way, shredding into a pulp that stained faintly under my hands. The sound was intimate, like bones crushed in miniature.

The smell rose sharp and green, a scent that clung to the back of my throat, medicinal and metallic all at once. It was not unpleasant. It was honest—this was the smell of endings disguised as beginnings.

I scraped the pulp into cheesecloth and pressed until liquid seeped through, gold-dark, catching the kitchen light in threads. My hands moved without hesitation, each step rehearsed in memory even though I'd never done this exact one before. Precision lived in me now.

When it was strained clean, I poured it into a glass jar. The liquid gleamed faintly, no different to the eye than herbal honey or some infusion from a high-end bar. I sealed the lid tight, wiped the rim twice, and labeled nothing. Secrets should never have names.

My chest tightened not with guilt but with certainty. The rehearsals were over. The finale had already begun.

As I pulled back into the venue lot, the night air softened. The lanterns along the main path glowed steadily, casting an amber glow over the gravel. The air was refreshingly cool, carrying the sweet scent of pine sap and the gentle hint of river water.

Everything looked brighter, fresher—more radiant.

It was the kind of night that pretended nothing bad could happen. That was the trouble with nights like this—they were liars. They let you breathe too easily, lulled you into thinking the ground was solid when it had been shifting under your feet all along.

Beyond the parking area, the trees swayed gently, their leaves whispering against each other in a soothing melody.

The main building loomed before me, its windows mostly dark, like a sleeping giant. Only a few windows still shone with a soft light, a testament to the revelers who refused to call it a night.

My phone buzzed in my pocket, snapping the scene in two.

I checked the phone—a message from Remmy flashing on the screen:

*You coming back to the hotel? House isn't that far... I need my bride. I'm still up watching TV.*

I replied quickly, reassuring him that I'd be back at the hotel soon. No need to worry. I slid the phone back into my pocket, my fingers brushing over the box again.

I had grabbed the jar and placed it in a shoebox, a loaded pistol in a 12 oz container.

Every step toward the door made the bag heavier, like it had its own rhythm. My wrist ached, but I didn't shift my grip—partly out of care, partly out of superstition.

But the moment I crossed that threshold inside the hotel lobby, every movement, every glance, would feel like it had weight. My breathing found a rhythm to match my steps—measured, deliberate.

My gaze fell on the bridal bag I carried in my other arm, its innocent masking the purpose of my run home. I'd placed pale roses and pink peonies, positioned perfectly to spill over the shoebox's edges, a clever disguise for the more deadly items hidden beneath. I'd checked them five times already, making sure everything was in place.

Inside the lobby, the atmosphere was quiet but not deserted. A bellhop wheeled a luggage cart toward the elevator, while a pair of bridesmaids from another wedding lounged on the sofa, their faces aglow in the soft light of their phones. A man at the desk argued with the receptionist about a late checkout, his voice rising in frustration. The air was thick with the scent of wood polish and the fading sweetness of someone's perfume.

I kept my expression neutral, my footsteps unhurried as I made my way to the elevator. I'd practiced this face before—soft eyes, relaxed mouth—

just enough warmth to look like someone who belonged here, but not enough to invite conversation.

My fingerprints felt like evidence, a careless mistake waiting to happen. The bridesmaids barely looked up, but I caught the man at the desk glancing toward me between sentences with the receptionist. I felt him clock the box—maybe not what was inside, but the care I was taking to keep it upright.

I forced my grip to loosen, afraid that a knuckle turning white might give me away. That was the goal—to blend in, to be invisible.

The ride to the second floor was empty, the elevator gliding upward in practiced silence. I leaned into the cool metal wall, counting in fours to steady my breathing. In the mirrored panel beside the doors, my reflection stared back, a mask of calmness.

When the doors slid open, I moved quickly, my heart pounding in anticipation. Left, then right. Room 214. And then—impact.

The box jolted hard, one of the peonies folding in on itself. My elbow smacked the wall, a jarring sensation that left me breathless. "Oh—Em?" Matt's voice, warm and familiar, broke the silence.

He caught the box before it could fall, a jar of death resting against his chest. The petals he grabbed with it looked bruised, like it had witnessed something it shouldn't.

His hand brushed the peonies' surface that covered my secret, and I swore he paused—just long enough to notice the faint herbal sweetness laced into the petals concealing something smellier inside. His cheeks were flushed, his eyes glassy but warm, his scent a heady mix of citrus and cologne. I imagined the bag slipping from his hands, the flowers spilling out, the small jar wrapped inside a plastic grocery bag tucked inside shifting into view.

My heart was still racing, but not from the bump. If his gaze lingered, I'd only smile—polite, steady, unreadable. I'd practiced that calm in mirrors until even I couldn't tell it was a mask.

I created a small, practiced smile, as usual. It felt stapled in place. "Sorry," I said, trying to play it cool.

Matt didn't notice, too caught up in his own apology. I reached for my items in his hand, a split-second too late. "Let me help—what room are you? Left? Right?" he asked, his voice cheerful.

I hesitated, my mind racing. "I've got it," I said finally, trying to retrieve the bag.

But Matt was already walking ahead, humming something off-key. I caught up just in time to see him plant the bag in front of my door like he was delivering groceries. "You sure you don't want to come down to the bar?" he asked, his smile faltering for a second.

Something flickered there—hesitation, maybe curiosity—but it was gone before I could name it. I wondered if he'd smelled the faint herbal sweetness clinging to the blooms, if it registered somewhere beneath the citrus and cologne. "Remmy's probably bouncing off the walls. He's not the type to sit still this long."

I shook my head, firm. "No, thanks," I said, trying to sound convincing. I didn't trust my voice to hold if I added anything else. Short sentences were safer—less room for the tremor to slip through.

Matt lingered for a beat too long, like he might press it, but then the elevator dinged. He lifted two fingers in a lazy salute and wandered toward it, his gait loose and lazy. Only when the doors closed did I let myself breathe again.

Inside, Remmy was propped against the pillows, the TV flickering in the dim light. "Hey," he said, setting the remote aside. "You okay?"

I nodded, keeping my voice light. "Just tired. A lot of stimulation today."

"Come to bed," he said, his voice soft. He was so easy in moments like this—soft edges, warm hands. A man who could make you forget the sharp parts. And that was the danger.

He reached for my hand, his touch warm and comforting. I sat with him for a minute, letting the quiet settle over us. "You're safe now," he murmured, not opening his eyes.

When his breathing evened out, I slipped from the bed and opened the box. The plants went in one corner of the suite, the miscellaneous décor items in another. The roots gritted inside the jar went into a smaller canvas bag in the nightstand drawer. It wouldn't look strange, just another herbal blend. Still, I slid it to the very back, beneath the lavender satchel the hotel had provided, so that even I would have to search for it.

I liked that. It gave me the illusion of control, like the danger was in another room entirely, waiting for me to call it in. Distance didn't just keep it hidden—it made me feel steadier, like I'd bought myself a little more time to decide. It was one thing to plan in abstract; another to have the pieces sitting in the same room as him.

I worked quietly, listening to the muffled sounds from the hallway. Laughter—female, high-pitched—from down the west wing. A door closing softly. The bridal party had mostly checked in earlier. Remmy's cousins, Mark and Aaron, both groomsmen, had rooms across from each other near the elevators. They were loud in a way that was somehow charming, always leaning too far into a story or roping someone into a card game in the lobby.

My bridesmaids were clustered a little further down: Jessica and Claire sharing a room, my sister-in-law-to-be Sara next door to them. Claire's laugh was easy to pick out, sharp, staccato, followed by a string of exaggerated *oh my Gods*. It made me smile without meaning to.

By the time I'd finished sorting everything, the hallway had gone still again. Even in their absence, the bridal party's noise clung to the hallway like perfume. The carpet muffled footsteps so well it was almost eerie. It felt like the kind of silence that holds its breath, waiting for something to happen. The kind of silence that makes you check the lock twice without knowing why.

Just before midnight, Remmy walked me down to my own suite, a tradition we hated but made Remmy's mom Marlene extra happy. The two wings mirrored each other, with thick carpet, identical sconces, and quiet paintings of mountain streams. We passed Mark in the hall, leaning halfway out of his door to tell us goodnight, and Aaron calling something muffled from inside.

At my door, Remmy hesitated. "Goodnight, Em," he said finally, leaning down to kiss my forehead. His voice was low, almost reverent, and he didn't even look over his shoulder to see if I'd gone in. The way he looked at me then made something in my chest ache—not from love, but from the reminder that trust could be this simple for him. He'd never learned the kind of trust that costs something. For him, it was as easy as closing his eyes and assuming the roof would still be over his head in the morning.

"Goodnight," I whispered.

I slipped inside, closing the door softly behind me. The suite smelled faintly of lavender from the sachets the staff had left on the pillows. I leaned against the door, let the quiet sink in, and—for the first time since I'd come upstairs—allowed myself to smile. It wasn't joy—it was recognition. All the pieces were finally in the same place.

Tomorrow, everything would happen exactly as planned.

Just not for the reasons anyone here expected.

# Chapter 13:

# Wedding Day

I woke before my alarm to the low hum of the building—pipes, vents, the soft click of someone's door down the hall. The room was dim and clean-edged, the kind of hotel darkness that made the window seem like a cutout.

For a few seconds I didn't move, listening to the quiet and measuring my own breathing against it. A morning where the air felt polite, as if it didn't want to disturb what was about to happen.

A text from Remmy was waiting on my phone.

*You up? Breakfast opens at 7. Meet you for something light in the lobby before?*

*Sure,* I typed back. *Five minutes.*

The air outside the bathroom felt cooler, touched by that faint eucalyptus note from the bouquet. It shouldn't have made me think of the jar of deathly roots, but it did—how its scent could lean medicinal or dangerous depending on the story you told yourself.

The therapist had texted a polite "checking in" last night. I'd deleted it unread—too soon for questions, too late for therapy.

In the mirror, my face looked rested. That was something. I smoothed the duvet once, out of habit, then slipped my keycard into my pocket and stepped into the hall.

Morning on the second floor lived in a whisper. A housekeeping cart rolled by in the distance; a bridesmaid laughed and shushed herself in the same breath. The thick carpet swallowed sound as I passed the framed photos—the retreat under snow; women with baskets of laundry in the courtyard; a line of chairs in an empty hall. All those rooms, all that quiet work.

Remmy was already at a two-top by the window, hands wrapped around a mug, his eyes soft with sleep. He stood when he saw me, the automatic courtesy he'd learned from his father and never questioned. It was easy to like him in these moments—easier still to forget the calendar of what came next.

"Hi," he said, kissing my forehead. "You okay?"

"I'm okay." I sat. "You?"

He grinned at the table like he couldn't help it. "We're getting married."

We ate eggs and toast and fruit while the lobby woke around us—vendors rolling cases, the florist's assistant wheeling buckets of stock and dusty miller, the coordinator in flats and a blazer, zipping around. Remmy told me a quick story about Mark's dream (lost tuxedo, tuxedo found in a freezer) and how Aaron had already ironed everyone's pocket squares because he "doesn't trust men with corners."

"Did you sleep?" he asked.

"Enough." I took a sip of coffee. "Hair and makeup are at nine. Claire texted me a list of lipsticks like she's arming for war."

He laughed. "Matt and I need to pick up a few things in town around ten. Cool if I disappear for an hour?"

I wanted to reach over the table, to grab him by his shirt. *You tell me this now?*

Instead, I smiled, pushing my eggs around my china plate.

"Of course," I said, lining the fork prongs with the rim of the plate. The small alignment trick kept my hands steady. "Just don't be late to the ceremony," I said, followed by a wink.

He raised both hands, mock surrender. "You can kill me if I am."

I smiled from the irony but let him feel proud of his joke.

We finished our meal, separating with a kiss.

"Today, you become Mrs. Black."

"I can't wait." *But our reasons couldn't be more different.*

By eight-thirty, the bridal suite buzzed with voices and curling irons. Jessica, Claire, Sara—faces bright, movements efficient. Their chatter skimmed the surface of the day while they painted and powdered me into the version of myself that would stand in front of hundreds.

They all looked at me like another bride in a parade of weddings. Smiling, ordinary, forgettable. They'd never suspect I was building something that would outlast all of theirs.

They didn't know they were dressing a bride and a killer.

"You're glowing," Claire said, adjusting the fall of my hair.

*If only she knew why.*

The rest of the pre-ceremony included photos with bridesmaids and Remmy's parents, who did their best to act normal in the absence of my parents.

"You look so beautiful, Emily," Chuck said, giving an awkward wave.

"Oh, Emily!" Marlene exclaimed, throwing her arms over me. "You look so beautiful. Should we take a photo for your mom?" She began digging through her purse.

I shot Claire a look, who nodded and stepped in. "We've sent her some already, she loved them! Let's all head downstairs. Photo time!"

My shoulders relaxed.

An hour of photos flew by—awkward poses and a struggle to stay cool in the blazing sun. A rotating list of 1:1s with bridesmaids, full bridal party, a shot with Remmy's mom and dad. It was hard to focus on the perfect pose when my mind was fixated on the perfect brew.

*This is delicious.* I could almost hear him now, his words taunting me. *I love this. Can you make me more?*

My thoughts were cut short by a tug, Remmy's niece showing off her small matching white gown.

"You look gorgeous, Lydia!" I bent down to meet her gaze, admiring the thin pieces of baby's breath braided into her hair.

A feeling I couldn't name—familiarity?—washed over me. The lights flashed twice, a small ringing straining my eardrum.

I looked at Lydia, but she wasn't Lydia anymore—it was a younger version of myself. I looked at my hands, a shadow misshaped around my hand. She tugged me again.

"Are you proud of me?" young me asked, looking at me with impatient eyes.

I studied her, a force washing over me like a blanket.

"Yes," I found myself saying. "You will do such a great job." I looked at my hands again, static hovering on and around them.

"Should I give him tea? Would that make you spend time with me again?" Young me smiled, her eyes bright with the possibilities.

A light too bright stung my eyes, the static disappearing from my vision.

I said, "Can I take my shoes off now?"

Young me was gone, shifted back into Lydia, who was now sitting on the floor, tugging at her shoes.

I blinked, grabbed a nearby water bottle and devoured it at once. My mind started to clear.

Lydia stood, running back down the hall, shouting for her mother. Her shoes dangled in either hand.

I wasn't my mother.

*I love Remmy. I want to give him a perfect night.*

I rubbed my temples and attempted to be present.

Photographers continued to snap photos, bridesmaids continued to orchestrate, but my mind was fixated.

By the time Remmy's text came—*Ready when you are*—I stared at the words for a long moment.

*Ready,* I typed back.

He meant walking down the aisle. I meant walking him to the edge of something final.

Twenty minutes until I'd see him. Six hours until our private dance.

Then, back to our room, where I'd brew his final tea.

But first, the cameras would catch me smiling, the guests would toast to our happiness, and people would celebrate our love.

Then, sometime after midnight, Remmy Black would learn what happens to men who think trust is unconditional.

---

The doors opened and the terrace brightened, like someone had quietly turned the world up a notch. The kind of light that makes skin look rinsed clean, that rounds off the edges of people's faces. The light seemed intentional, choosing its subjects, deciding where to settle.

Chairs sat in neat rows. The hedges were squared, ruler-perfect. Beyond them, the lake held its breath, surface flat as if even water knew when to keep still. The air had that strange, anticipatory hush that makes you believe everything—even the landscape—is listening.

I stepped out onto the stone, counting in fours. My heels clicked once, then hushed themselves as though the terrace had swallowed the sound. Somewhere behind me, a chair shifted. A faint whiff of hairspray mingled with the powdery green of clipped boxwood. Every detail—timed, balanced—felt like it had been orchestrated for me alone, for this one measured walk.

Dana's timing lived in my spine. The quartet's bows moved in disciplined arcs, their rhythm as rigid as a pulse. A breeze teased the hem of my dress, then stilled itself. Faces blurred to soft shapes until they resolved: Marlene dabbing at her eye, Chuck standing taller than he needed to, Mark and Aaron half-smiling as if they were suppressing a grin.

Remmy stood at the end of the aisle, hands clasped. His shoulders were a fraction tighter than usual, but when he caught sight of me, his mouth softened into the expression that once convinced me he believed in permanence.

The officiant began. His voice carried the practiced warmth of someone who'd been marrying strangers for years but still wanted to mean it. I heard the scaffolding beneath his words—the calculated pauses, the lines engineered to fold neatly into applause, the phrasing built for photographs. I stood where I'd been told. Remmy's fingers brushed mine, then held, light but sure.

The vows were familiar—words we'd both heard, both mocked, both agreed on. Rehearsed or not, saying them made them heavier. During the ring exchange, Remmy pretended to have lost his band, patting his shoe with a grin, until I reached into his jacket pocket and produced the ring like a magician's assistant pulling off the final trick. Relief rippled through the crowd. The quartet held a cadence while the lake tossed back a sheet of light.

"By the authority vested in me..." The officiant's voice stretched out over stone and water. "I now pronounce you—"

We kissed. His lips were steady, warm with faint traces of champagne and soap. It felt like he was sealing something he already owned.

Applause came first, polite. Then the noise surged, too loud for the space, as if the crowd needed volume to confirm that something irreversible had happened. Confetti wands cracked open—biodegradable, Dana had insisted—and soft paper drifted down like a managed weather system. We walked back up the aisle, into the bright rectangle of the doors, and the building swallowed us with its cool, polished breath.

Inside, the terrace's heat clung to my skin, but the air was crisp enough to raise goosebumps. My dress whispered across the floor. My heart, which had kept tempo down the aisle, still counted in fours.

Relief arrived first. Then logistics. People moved in, eager to help, because they always do after they've watched you endure something public. Marlene pressed water into my hand. Claire fluffed an imaginary wrinkle in my sleeve. Jessica bent to unhook a shoe snag I hadn't felt. Their gestures were small but persistent, like they were reassuring themselves I was tangible.

The photographer took over, efficient as a conductor. She moved us from light to shade, to a corner beneath an old window. "Family first," she said. They arranged themselves instinctively: Marlene to my left, Chuck anchoring the opposite side, Remmy centered. Matt hovered at the edge, slipping in and out of the frame like a cautious moon orbiting the picture. When our eyes met, his smile was almost ordinary— but he held it half a second too long. The camera clicked like a clock keeping score.

By the time cocktail hour began, the terrace had remade itself. High-top tables dotted the stone like punctuation. Servers floated past with champagne flutes and food too delicate to have names. Guests migrated toward the lake as if pulled. The quartet softened into a cheerful, expensive background.

People touched my arm constantly. They said we looked "meant to be." They told stories Remmy didn't remember and stories I didn't want to. My laugh sounded correct. My smile held. The dress obeyed. From a distance, Dana's clipboard flashed like a tiny sun.

Jessica slipped me a canapé, whispering, "Eat. Pictures lie about blood sugar." I obeyed. Smoke from the kitchen curled briefly through the air, then vanished. The servers refreshed glasses on repeat. I watched champagne become a habit in people's hands. Hand them bubbles often enough, and they'll stop paying attention.

Remmy's hand stayed at the small of my back, steady as a pilot light. He introduced me to cousins' bosses, to coaches, to aunts who swore they knew me. He was fluent at this—translating strangers into a table, blending disparate lives without anyone feeling misplaced. Every so often he glanced at me, quick, checking, and I'd answer with the small nod that meant: *still here.*

From the corner of my vision, I caught Ms. Volkova near the hedge. She stood at its edge like punctuation, posture composed, her navy dress neat but unshowy. Our eyes met, and she gave the barest incline of her head—not approval, not warmth, but accuracy: *You are where you said you'd be.* She didn't smile. She didn't need to.

Her gaze skimmed the crowd, marking exits, never lingering too long. But when it passed over me again, I felt its weight settle into my chest like a stone.

The evening pulled itself along in practiced transitions. Group photos blurred into a receiving line; circles formed and broke. Mark told a joke that made a table roar, then wince at their own volume. Aaron caught a glass before it shattered. Marlene tucked another nonexistent hair behind my ear. Everyone busied themselves with holding things together.

Music changed. The DJ tested volume that hummed without shouting. His assistant checked wires like arteries. The ballroom doors opened, and bodies flowed inside, the temperature climbing with them. The chandeliers caught the new arrivals, scattering light like glass rain.

The room was built to flatter.

We waited at the threshold, the DJ's hand hovering over the fader. Names rippled through the room as the bridal party performed their practiced entries—small spins, half bows, laughter rehearsed but convincing.

"And now," the DJ's voice warmed, "for the first time—"

The room turned, clapped. The noise was a blanket. We walked in, and the fit was seamless.

The last time Remmy would ever be announced as husband. Or at all.

At the sweetheart table, a server replaced our water and set down two fresh champagne flutes. I lifted one, watched the bubbles ladder the side, then set it back down, unsipped. The clock on the DJ's laptop glowed in its dark nest of cables. Time had been obedient all day. It would continue to be. The clock's green digits looked harmless too—just numbers—but they were the spine of the night.

7:42 p.m. Open dancing started twelve minutes ago.

"After the last song," I reminded myself silently, trying to resist the urge to grab the tea now. I wanted to touch it, smell it, remind myself it was there.

After the last song, I'd brew the tea. Valerian root to sweeten, the ground flower hidden in the blend I'd perfected until no one could see the difference. A curl of steam—looking exactly like every other curl of steam. A smile rehearsed enough to look unrehearsed. A widow's grief that would land in the right register because I had practiced it until I could summon it like breath.

I had practiced more than that. I'd practiced aftermaths—the scripts, the questions, the quiet version of myself who would answer them.

In the quiet hours, I'd even written lines in my head: the widow of a doctor, married only one night, telling her story. The book no one could look away from. The tragedy that made me permanent.

It wasn't guilt that rose in me as I thought of it—it was focus. A thrill that sharpened my smile until people commented on how radiant I looked.

I *was* radiant. I was ready.

And yet—eyes.

I felt them before I found them. Matt, leaning back at the bar, posture casual, drink in hand. He wasn't glaring, wasn't even frowning. He was just... watching.

Steady, unhurried, the way someone keeps an eye on a low flame.

He lifted his phone once, like he was checking the time, but the flash reflection caught glass. A photo—proof, or leverage, I couldn't tell which.

The sight reminded me—not shock, not revelation, but the old truth: paranoia was oxygen. He had been noticing, and would again. I tore my gaze back to Remmy, pressed my knee against his under the table, forcing my body to stay with him.

His laugh rose above the music, warm and unknowing, and I tried to let it pull me back into the role.

*Focus on Remmy. Focus on the plan.*

# Chapter 14:

# May I Have This Dance?

The hand on my shoulder turned the world cold before I even heard his voice.

"Can I steal a dance?"

My stomach dropped as though someone had yanked a string inside me. I pasted on a smile, glancing at Remmy. He hesitated, but only for a beat—then made a gesture of approval with the unbothered grace of someone who trusted too much.

Matt motioned towards me, his hand taking mine, the other resting at my waist once we found the dancefloor. Not close enough to raise eyebrows, not distant enough to be platonic. He didn't pull me in. He pressed. The weight of his palm felt like a nail driven through fabric.

"You look beautiful," he said. His voice had the appropriate warmth, the kind that other people would hear and find flattering. But his eyes didn't match his tone. They were too sharp, too careful, the kind that filed details away in some secret ledger.

"Thank you," I said, my smile easy, practiced. My dress whispered against his suit as we swayed. "It's been a perfect day."

"Has it?"

The question hung there like a hook. Not sharp enough to wound in public, but sharp enough to snag.

Matt laughed too loudly, the grip of his fingers tightening on the small of my back.

"Don't worry," he said with a look that said he believed he'd already won. "I'll go easy on you."

I blinked, steadying my breath. "What do you mean?"

"Nothing," he said, smiling—too smooth. "Just checking that you're actually happy. Not performing happy."

Performing. The word sank its teeth in. His hand pressed against my spine like he was feeling for the exact spot where my lies lived.

"I'm very happy," I replied, the lie fluid on my tongue, my face arranging itself without thought. I had practiced this expression, hadn't I? With Remmy, with the therapist, with everyone who needed to believe.

Matt's eyes didn't soften. He swayed with me, rhythm steady, posture perfect, as if the music was only cover for interrogation.

The quartet's violins swelled, and the crowd blurred to the edges of my vision. I could only see him. His pupils dilated slightly as if testing me, and I wondered what he thought he might find.

I tried to push his words out of my mind, tried to focus on the light touch of his hand, on the way people clapped along for couples twirling nearby. But his voice was in my ear again, quieter this time.

"Remmy deserves the real thing," he said.

It was almost kind, almost gentle. Almost.

But it wasn't kind—it was a warning dressed as concern.

I forced a laugh, shaking my head like he'd said something silly. "Of course he does. And he has it."

"I would do anything for Remmy," Matt murmured. "Anything."

I focused on my reaction, forcing my eyes and lips to refrain from quivering.

The music dipped lower, the kind of song chosen to let couples lean in close. I didn't. I kept the polite space between us, but Matt's hand at my waist made the air feel thinner, like he was slowly closing a vice.

"You've been... tired lately, haven't you?" he said, tone light enough that someone overhearing might think it casual. But his thumb pressed against the fabric at my side with each syllable. "Planning a wedding takes a lot out of a person."

I smiled, tilting my head, a perfect imitation of the relaxed bride. "It does. That's why I've been leaning on Remmy so much. He's been incredible."

"Mm," Matt said, the sound sitting somewhere between agreement and skepticism.

My pulse stuttered. He couldn't know—not exactly. He was too careful to accuse outright. He was leaving open space for me to fill.

"You're overthinking, Matt. We're all just tired."

The corners of his mouth twitched upward. It wasn't a smile—it was the acknowledgment of a point scored. He leaned slightly closer, his voice soft enough that only I could hear:

"You've always been precise. Too precise. People notice."

For a moment, the music faded. The chandelier light blurred. All I could see was Matt's steady gaze, the quiet certainty in it. Not accusation yet—diagnosis.

I wanted to pull away. I didn't. To step back would be to admit there was something to fear. So I held my ground, gliding us through another turn on the dance floor. My smile widened, teeth flashing in the candlelight. "Maybe that's why this wedding looks so perfect. Precision pays off."

Matt's hand didn't move, but his grip felt heavier. "You scare me sometimes, Emily. No one stays that calm when everything's changing."

The song's chords stretched out like a held breath. Around us, other couples spun and laughed, oblivious to the fact that a war was being fought in whispers and half-smiles.

I didn't answer him. Not directly. Instead, I tilted my head toward the sweetheart table where two untouched champagne flutes glittered in the candlelight.

"Did he tell you he's been seeing a cardiologist?"

My eyes snapped up to meet his.

*Cardiologist?*

I'd seen his paperwork from the doctor, but a specialist suggested he took another step into his suspicion.

"He's been twice in the last month." He stared at me while we danced like a hawk eyeing its prey. "He didn't tell you because he didn't want to add to your stress."

His eyes followed mine, a smirk resting on his face. He stared long enough for my chest to clench.

"He has heart failure in his lineage." I stood taller, taking the lead in our dance. "We just completed our family genealogy and genetic history. It's riddled in his bloodline—I was the one who first pushed him to make the appointment," I lied, clenching for the potential he'd catch me in my lie.

His expression was unreadable again. But something flickered there—knowledge, maybe. Or the patience of someone who intended to wait until the exact moment the mask slipped.

"You noticed his color lately?" Matt asked. "Kind of pale, like he hasn't been sleeping."

"He's fine," I said too quickly.

"Maybe. Still…" He softened, like a boy begging for candy. "Come on. All of his best friends are here, staying in a rental together—let him come spend the night with us… let us keep an eye on him."

The words *keep an eye on him* cut like a blade.

"I asked him, you know," Matt murmured, leaning into my ear. "He said he'd really like that, wouldn't want to hurt your feelings, though…"

"Remmy didn't say that," I cut sharp.

"Oh really?" His eyes lifted. "Did he tell you that? Just like he told you about the cardiologist?"

Right before the music ended, I noticed Ms. Volkova watching me from her dinner table, next to neighbors whose gestures suggested they were gossiping.

But she sat next to them, focused on me and Matt. Her eyes held the same look as Matt's—two hawks eyeing the pantry of their Earth.

Her face quickly flashed to mine before returning to Matt—I could have sworn I saw her wink.

The music cut just in time, where I let my hands fall from his shoulders as if I were simply returning to my husband. Matt stood, expression blank. To anyone watching, it had been a sweet dance between friends.

I kept my eye contact as I walked away, letting him break first.

But my skin burned where his hand had rested, as if he'd branded me with suspicion.

The band's song slowed into something syrupy, and Remmy's hands found me again.

"Seriously, Em, you look beautiful," he said, his voice unguarded, almost boyish as he swayed us back into rhythm.

I leaned into him, trying to keep him from feeling the vibration in my body.

"Thank you." I studied Remmy's face the way I used to study blueprints—scanning for cracks in the foundation, looking for what he might actually see when he looked at me. "It's been a perfect day."

But my body was still humming with the aftertaste of Matt's presence, that earlier dance where his fingers had felt like pins in my back. I'd walked away intact, face steady, lies neat, and yet my skin still buzzed with the phantom pressure. He hadn't cornered me, hadn't named anything—but something in the way his eyes pierced mine made me aware of the acid in my stomach.

I tried to reassure myself.

I had smiled. I had held. I had won.

I repeated it over and over again, covering the echoing of Matt's voice in my ears: *I won*. I let my cheek rest against Remmy's shoulder.

Matt could watch all he wanted; it didn't matter. I was the one writing the ending.

And my plan was precise, measured... perfect.

Then the music shifted again, and my pulse skipped.

The faint trace of clove cut through the champagne and sugar, sharp enough to turn my head before I even saw her.

Out on the dance floor, impossibly, was Ms. Volkova—my pale-blue-eyed neighbor, elegant as ever, moving with grace that seemed borrowed from another era.

And guiding her through a waltz with startling confidence was, of all guests, Matt.

For a moment, I couldn't place the sight: Volkova in silk, her hand curved lightly over his shoulder; Matt, usually stiff as a servant, leading her with practiced assurance; his steps fluid, his posture relaxed.

"Well, would you look at that," Remmy's voice slid in behind my ear, warm with champagne. His arms tightened around my waist as we both watched.

Volkova said something, lips close to Matt's ear, and he laughed—a real laugh, not the tight professional one he usually offered me. For a fleeting moment, he looked younger, softened, almost human.

"Think they'll hook up later?" Remmy whispered, wicked humor slipping into his tone. "The mysterious widow and the suspicious firefighter—tell me that's not the setup for the strangest romance novel you've ever heard."

The comment startled a laugh out of me, sharp and genuine. "Remmy!"

"What? Look at them. She's practically glowing, and he's got that dopey smile that only comes out when he's actually having fun instead of scanning everyone like suspects."

I turned to look at him fully, surprised by his irreverence. This, this playful Remmy, was the man I'd first fallen for—the one before the corrections, before the quiet dismissals.

"You're terrible," I said, but my lips curved anyway.

"I'm observant," he corrected, spinning me lazily so we could both watch as Matt guided Ms. Volkova into a dramatic dip. She let herself fold into it with surprising trust, and when he pulled her upright, applause rippled through the crowd.

They bowed to each other theatrically, a performance that charmed the guests into laughter. Someone clapped too hard; someone else called for an encore. Neither offered one.

Instead, Ms. Volkova leaned in close. Her hand brushed Matt's arm with the intimacy of someone who already knew him better than the rest of us did. Her lips moved with words I couldn't catch. Matt bent his head, listening.

That was not a performance. That was communication.

"Are they...?" I began, but Remmy was already grinning, smug.

"Yep. Look at that. Twenty minutes of dancing and he's completely smitten." He gestured toward them with his glass as Matt, uncharacteristically deferential, offered Volkova his arm. She accepted without hesitation, and the two moved off the floor together.

Not back to her table. Not toward the cluster of laughing guests. They walked in tandem toward the edge of the room, then further, toward the bar's shadowed alcove. Their heads bent together as if sharing something private, their bodies aligned as though they'd practiced.

"Probably off to get a drink," Remmy said, self-satisfied. "Told you. By the end of the night, Volkova's going to have a very dedicated admirer."

I nodded, eyes tracking them until the pair disappeared around the corner.

But my thoughts weren't light or teasing. They were sharp, needle-fine.

Volkova—who had handed me roots with quiet instruction, who had told me dosage mattered most of all. Matt—who had danced with me like a warning, whose eyes had dared me to slip. Now the two of them together, close, sharing words no one else could hear.

The room blurred back into focus around me—the DJ's bass line, the chatter, the scrape of cutlery—but I felt that absence like a gap in the floorboards. They were gone. And I didn't know what, or who, they were conspiring about.

"Maybe you're right," I told Remmy, smiling just enough.

But inside, the certainty re-solidified. Tonight would still be mine. Matt could laugh, Volkova could whisper—but I'd already chosen the ending.

I found an excuse to slip away—an easy task for a bride on her wedding day. The second dress in my closet was the perfect excuse. "I'll be back... need to freshen up," I'd whispered to Remmy, giving him a seductive look that implied, *maybe I'll come back with something you'll like.*

The elevator carried me up to our floor in blessed quiet, the reception's noise fading to a muffled thump below. Soon, I'd have everything I needed. The second dress hanging in the closet. The cosmetics bag with its twin sachets. And Remmy, relaxed and unsuspecting, ready for the perfect end to our perfect day.

I rounded the corner toward our suite, already reaching for the key card—

And stopped dead.

Someone was coming out of our room.

Not the adjoining room, not a similar door down the hall.

Our room.

Matt stepped into the hallway and turned away from me, heading toward the other elevator bank. He moved quickly, purposefully, like someone who'd completed a task. He never looked in my direction.

He'd been inside our room—either to look, to take, or to leave something I hadn't planned for.

I pressed myself against the wall, watching him disappear around the corner.

All the while my heart hammered against my ribs.

# Chapter 15:

# Goodnight

When I finally swiped my key card and slipped inside, the suite was exactly as we'd left it. Bed made. Shoes lined up. Remmy's tie draped across the bench at the foot of the bed.

I crossed to my bag, moving slowly, as if speed might startle whatever I was about to find. I unzipped the side pocket—the one only I used—and there it was: the linen pouch.

Still sealed. Still where I'd left it.

But not *how* I'd left it.

Something in me flinched, the way you do when you wake in the dark certain you've heard your name whispered. The drawer looked like it had been put back together by someone trying to mimic order but not understanding it. Like a stranger making your bed.

It wasn't the mess that unsettled me—it was the imitation of order. Like a child's drawing of a house— recognizable, but wrong in ways you sensed before you could name. The way someone had tried to return things exactly as they thought I'd left them, and failed.

I remembered tucking it flat, zipping the pouch, burying it under two layers of silk wrap and my backup lipstick. I always did it the same way. Everything in its place.

Now the pouch was angled differently. The silk had shifted. The lipstick was upside down.

I opened the pouch. The vials were all intact. Untouched.

And yet—wrong.

I stood there for a long time, pouch in hand, replaying my memory like a tape. What had been different?

It was like a children's book, to spot the difference between two images. I couldn't name what wasn't right—perhaps the way the inner plastic bag was laying.

My pulse thumped against the inside of my skull, hot and pounding. I told myself to breathe, to think rationally, but my mind was already running in a hundred directions.

Flashbacks darted in and out—Matt laughing with Ms. Volkova, their bodies too close, then the two of them slipping off the dance floor together. But when I saw him in the hallway... he was alone. Where was she?

The absence landed harder than her presence ever could. She was the kind of woman you noticed in every room—if she wasn't in sight, it meant she was somewhere she wanted more.

My head was hazy, my body too warm. Bile crept up the back of my throat.

Why was Matt alone in our room?

A knock down the hall startled me—laughter, glass clinking.

My chest tightened, the air in the suite suddenly too heavy. I'd built my whole night around control, and now, just like that, the edges were starting to fray.

I rewrapped the silk, capped the lipstick, and placed the pouch exactly where it should be. I zipped it, smoothed the silk over it, and shut the drawer with a careful click.

Good enough.

I changed into my second outfit and forced my body into performance mode—shoulder blades easing down, spine lengthening, mouth curving into the calm, practiced smile people expected from me tonight.

The smile was muscle memory now, a mask I could wear over anything—fear, rage, guilt. From the outside, no one would see the difference.

Back in the ballroom, the music swelled—a different kind of loud now, the polished elegance of earlier giving way to the messy, loose edges of late night. People were laughing too hard, hugging too tightly.

I scanned the crowd.

I couldn't find Matt.

Ms. Volkova was missing too.

A strong arm slid around my waist. "Oh my god," Remmy said, pulling back to look at me. "You changed." His eyes scanned the dress—the cut, the fabric, the way the light caught on the silk—and I saw the exact moment he noticed every detail I'd hoped he would.

"You like?" I managed. My voice sounded almost normal.

"Like? I love. You're unreal," he said, spinning me toward the dance floor just as a slow song was starting. He spun me onto the dance floor, and I let myself be swept into the crowd, each step a negotiation between appearances and truth. He was warm from drinking, singing quietly in my ear as we swayed.

His palm spread over my back like a shield. Every time his thumb swept against my spine, I felt a flicker of the girl who said yes without hesitation. That girl didn't belong here tonight, but she was stubborn enough to keep showing up.

I tried to hold onto the moment, but my body was betraying me—the stumble in my step, the uneven breathing, the gnawing awareness in my stomach. Alcohol. Anxiety. Adrenaline.

"What's wrong?" he murmured, brow brushing mine.

"Nothing," I lied. "Just... been a long night."

I let my cheek rest against his shoulder, then pulled back slightly, forcing a casual tone. "Oh—hey. Weird thing. My keycard stopped working earlier. The desk person mentioned more than three cards had been checked out for our room. Did you grab two?"

He didn't hesitate. "Yeah, I gave one to Matt. I asked him to put the card box in our room—you know, the one with the cards and the cash tips for the vendors. Safer up there than in the lobby."

Relief never came clean; it always dragged a little grit with it. A part of me still waited for the other shoe to drop.

It was plausible. He could have been putting the box away. That could explain the key.

But it doesn't explain anything about why my pouch was disturbed.

The music carried us through the rest of the song. I smiled when I needed to, laughed at the right beats, even let him spin me once before the night's final exit. Inside, though, my thoughts stayed sharp and restless, circling the same question no matter how hard I tried to smooth it over.

*What did Matt see?*

The music pulsed warm and low, the kind of late-night playlist meant to keep the dance floor moving. My dress felt lighter now, the fabric whispering over my skin as I moved, smiling when people looked, nodding at whatever they said. I was doing it—passing.

But inside, my thoughts spun.

I swallowed hard, heat rising under my collarbone. Nausea fizzed in my stomach, a sour churn that felt like acid. My head was heavier than it should've been. My steps didn't feel entirely my own.

The dizziness passed as quickly as it came, replaced by that cold, surgical kind of alertness I trusted more than calm.

I scanned the room, willing an answer into existence. I wanted to lay my eyes on Matt, to look at his expression after leaving our room. No sign of him or Ms. Volkova anywhere.

Remmy's hands found my waist again from behind, and I startled, almost spilling what was left in my glass. "Hey," he murmured against my ear. "You okay? You've been in your head."

I shook it off, forcing a smile. "Long night. Great night. Just... a lot."

"Then let's call it," he said, lips brushing my temple. "We don't need the big private last dance if you're not feeling it. That's our thing, right? Do it our way."

I searched his face, the warmth in his eyes both comforting and dangerous. He'd believe anything I told him right now.

"Yeah?" I said, setting my glass on the nearest table. "Really?"

He grinned, laced his fingers through mine, and led me off the floor toward the elevator. I kept my back straight, my smile steady, but inside, my stomach was a knot of relief and unease.

A new, slow-burning kind of paranoia started— less about what happened, and more about who was watching me notice.

We stepped into the elevator, the mirrored walls catching our reflection from every angle—perfect couple, perfect night. His arm was still warm around my waist, grounding me even as my mind worked overtime.

By the time we reached our floor, my pulse had slowed, my panic folding into something manageable. Maybe it was nothing. Maybe I'd imagined more than was there.

Inside the suite, Remmy loosened his tie and went straight for the minibar. "Nightcap?" he asked, already pouring himself a double of something amber.

I nodded absently, scanning the room with a practiced casualness. "Where'd Matt put the cards?" I asked, my voice light.

"Oh—yeah," he said, swirling the liquor in his glass. "I asked him to stick them in a drawer. Safer than leaving them out for a housekeeper to grab." His tone was easy, but his eyes flickered toward the drawer under the TV, like a man checking the lock on a door he swore he'd closed.

The words landed with a small thud in my chest. It explained part of it. Not all. That was the danger of partial answers—they kept you in the room, but never let you sit down. They let you hang your fear on something flimsy and call it stable.

And flimsy things break loudest when you've convinced yourself they'll hold.

Still, I couldn't go straight for the drawer I really wanted. That would be too obvious, too eager. Instead, I took my time to mosey over—first I stood by the desk, a brisk pass by the minibar—pausing to comment idly on the view from the window, the music Remmy was queuing on the speaker, the way the gas fireplace flickered to life in the corner.

Finally, with his back turned, I slid open the drawer.

There, on the right-hand side, was the neat stack of card envelopes.

I stared for a beat longer than I needed to. A cool washed over me. Enough to make me feel ridiculous for the spiral I'd just had.

The story gained logic as my emotions dialed down. Matt came into the room to put away our cards. No one stopped me, no big alarms. I started to convince myself the pouch was never touched at all, that paranoia infected my memory.

I closed the drawer and turned toward Remmy, who was holding out a hand. "Dance with me," he said, voice low but insistent.

There was no music yet, but the speaker crackled as something slow and rich began to play—Sam Cooke, warm and timeless. He pulled me in, one hand at my waist, the other settling between my shoulder blades. I let myself sink into it, breathing him in. One last private dance for the night.

"You were glowing out there," he murmured, lips brushing my hairline.

I smiled into his chest, letting the warmth in his voice melt a little of the tension in mine. "It's easy when I have the perfect partner."

We swayed until the song faded, our movements slowing even further until we were almost still.

"Tea?" I asked when the music stopped.

He groaned softly, heading toward the bed. "If you're making it. Sleepytime, please."

I laughed, the irony sitting just between my teeth. "Coming right up."

Ordinary wives vanish into casseroles and school pick-ups. Widows live forever in whispers, etched into the air of every room they enter.

The little kitchenette in the corner felt too bright compared to the low glow of the fireplace. I filled the kettle and set it on the burner, the quiet hiss of water hitting metal oddly loud in the otherwise soft room.

I peeked in the attached bedroom where Remmy stretched out on the bed, shoes off, shirt half unbuttoned. He looked almost boyish like that—loose, unguarded. His arm was draped over his eyes, the glass from his nightcap still on the side table.

I quietly tiptoed to where I'd left my pouch—still laying there like a dare—and pulled out the jar of roots I'd muddled. I held like I'd rehearsed, as if my hands already knew the steps.

The contents inside caught the light for just a second before I added it into the dry mug. The scent of mint and chamomile rose immediately.

After weeks of planning, the ending finally belonged to me.

I leaned against the counter, my pulse steadying for the first time since I'd seen Matt in that hallway. Tonight was still mine. The plan was still intact.

My fingers hesitated on the grip of the mug long enough for the thought to form: I could leave it. I could make the tea clean and still have the night end warm.

Then I remembered the betrayals—the time Remmy ordered the wrong flowers, the way he defied social norms by open-mouth chewing—and the hesitation vanished.

"Remember our first trip to New Orleans?" Remmy's voice was muffled from the bed, but I could hear the smile in it. "You swore that café was putting something in your tea because you couldn't keep your eyes open after two sips."

I let out a small laugh, tearing open a second packet for myself. "Maybe they were just better at brewing than you think."

The kettle whistle started, thin at first, then sharp. I poured in the hot water, watching the liquid darken and swirl, the powder already invisible. Every part of the tea-making was deliberate—the sound of the pour, the swirl of the liquid, the way steam rose and curled toward the bed like a messenger.

I didn't rush it. If it was going to happen, it should happen clean. Precise.

When I brought his to the bed, he sat up, hair mussed, the lines around his eyes softer now. "My beautiful wife," he said, taking the cup like it was the best gift he'd been handed all night.

It almost made me stop. Almost.

He accepted it—accepted the tea under all his suspicion. Against the advice of his best friend, his doctor, and whatever part of his brain was supposed to keep him cautious. Alcohol helped soften that filter.

I curled onto the bed beside him with my own cup, letting the heat soak into my palms.

He took a long sip, eyes closing briefly. "Perfect," he murmured.

A faint tremor ran through his fingers as he set the mug down—small enough to dismiss, but I catalogued it in my mind anyway.

*Onset: five minutes.*

He leaned back against the headboard, gently taking my mug from me and pulling me in so my head rested on his chest. His heartbeat was steady under my ear, the slow rhythm syncing with the faint pop of the fireplace.

We stayed like that for a while. I tried not to watch him too closely, but my eyes kept tracing the details— the way his shoulders eased, the tiny twitch in his jaw like his body was deciding whether to stay awake.

At one point, he yawned. Just a small one, quickly covered by another sip of tea. He laughed under his breath. "Guess the champagne's catching up to me."

My stomach fluttered—not nerves now, but something closer to satisfaction.

The flutter turned sharp, settling high under my ribs. My skin felt electric, like my pulse couldn't decide if it belonged to me or to him.

The room felt warmer, softer, the edges of the night closing in. He finished his tea, set the cup down, and stretched, his movements a little slower than usual. "Okay, Mrs. Black," he said, voice low, "it's time for bed."

I smiled, the grin coming easily now. "Goodnight, my husband."

He grinned and brushed a kiss against my hair before sliding under the covers. I stayed sitting on the edge of the bed for a moment, watching him settle in.

His breathing evened out faster than I expected. Not asleep—not yet—but the shift was there: the looseness, the way his eyelids lightly twitched.

I slipped deeper under the covers beside him, close enough to feel his warmth, and let my eyes close too.

For now, I could rest.

The plan was in motion. Tomorrow, everything would be different. His breath evened out so quickly it startled me. Not sleep, not yet—just the kind of surrender people only give when they're certain the person beside them will keep them safe. My chest tightened, but my hand stayed steady against the blanket.

The plan was alive. For now, so was he.

Until he closed his eyes.

Until death do us part.

# Chapter 16:

# Dream

The house stretches too long, hallways bending into endless corridors of mirrors. Every reflection shows me draped in black—veiled, delicate, admired. My footsteps echo like applause, though no one claps.

The kitchen door opens into a chapel. Rows of mourners line the counters, shoulders bowed, their whispers soft as moth wings: *Emily. Poor, poor Emily.* The sound makes the walls swell with breath.

A casket waits where the table should be, not wood but carved from flowers—oleander, monkshood, bleeding hearts spilling petals as if the blooms can't contain their grief. Their perfume clings thick to my lungs, sweet as honey and suffocating as smoke.

I step forward and the crowd parts, eyes shining. Someone reaches for my hand, another for my veil. I let them. Every touch is a confirmation, every lowered voice another thread weaving me into legend. I am tragedy incarnate. I am unforgettable.

At the casket's edge, I see myself reflected again— pale, trembling just enough to look fragile, beautiful in suffering. The kind of woman who earns casseroles delivered to her door, who makes neighbors drop their voices, who becomes a myth before she grows old.

I smile beneath the veil, unseen. A queen crowned with grief. A bride made holy by loss.

Then the lid shifts. A hand presses upward, pale fingers splitting the flowers apart. Gasps ripple through the crowd. The chapel tilts. The crown slips from my head.

The casket groans as though it might open.

I woke with the taste of soil in my mouth.

The ceiling above me was too white to be heaven. The smell of lilies still clung to my hands. My throat burned—not from soil, but from the silence that followed everyone's condolences. For a moment I couldn't tell if I was still in the dream or the wake.

Even awake, I could still feel the weight of that crown pressing into my skull.

# Chapter 17:

## Soil on My Tongue

I woke to a stillness that felt wrong, artificial, similar to the silence that follows an explosion when your ears are still ringing but the world has gone quiet around the devastation. The light filtering through the hotel curtains was soft and golden, the kind of morning illumination that suggested peace and new beginnings rather than the darker possibilities that had occupied my thoughts throughout the night.

The taste of soil still clung to my tongue. The perfume of flowers lingered in my nose, though the room only smelled faintly of champagne and hotel linens. Somewhere inside me, the echoes of a crown—the widow's crown I had worn in my sleep—slipped off my head before I could secure it.

Yet something was wrong. Too perfect, too staged—like the hush after a funeral hymn that ends too soon. For a breathless moment I kept my eyes shut, caught between the dream of black veils and whispered prayers and the reality pressing against my skin.

Beside me, Remmy's body was motionless in a way that made my chest tighten with equal parts hope and dread. This was the moment I had planned for months:

waking to find the poison had finished its work, that the grief I had rehearsed was no longer fantasy but fact.

For a breathless moment, I kept my eyes shut, afraid to look. My right foot rested against the back of his calf, and I concentrated on that point of contact. I felt for the warmth and subtle responsiveness that belonged to living tissue, for the unconscious micro-movements that bodies made even in the deepest sleep.

The muscle beneath my toes felt solid, substantial, radiating the kind of heat that suggested active circulation and metabolic function. Still warm. Still responsive to pressure. Still displaying all the characteristics that belonged to a living person.

Too warm for death. Too responsive for the kind of permanent stillness I'd expected to find after hours of alkaloid-induced cardiac disruption.

Then—movement. A subtle shift in the mattress that indicated changing position, the unconscious adjustment of Remmy transitioning from deep sleep toward wakefulness. I felt his muscle flex under my foot.

My chest seized with a disappointment so acute it felt like physical pain, like someone had reached inside my ribcage and squeezed my heart.

He was still alive.

Somewhere in the hall, a vacuum started, steady and oblivious. The world kept moving, ignorant of the crime that hadn't happened.

"Rem?" The name slipped out before I could stop it, carrying more weight than a simple morning greeting should bear, loaded with questions I couldn't ask directly and expectations I couldn't acknowledge openly.

Silence for a half beat that stretched long enough for me to imagine different endings, alternative realities where my voice would echo unanswered in a room that suddenly contained one living person instead of two.

Then the low, satisfied moan surfacing from the kind of profound rest that leaves you feeling restored and energetic rather than groggy and disoriented. He stretched like a man who'd slept better than he had in months, his movements fluid and confident in ways that should have been impossible if his nervous system had spent the night processing cardiac glycosides and other compounds designed to disrupt the normal functioning of vital organs.

He was not only alive—he was thriving. Radiating the kind of vitality that suggested perfect health.

The realization hit me with the force of a physical blow. Not only had my carefully researched, methodically prepared, precisely measured poison failed to kill him again, it seemed to be having the opposite effect entirely. All that research, all that precision—and I couldn't even outsmart a heart that refused to stop beating.

Heat flushed my face as my brain scrambled through increasingly desperate explanations. Wrong plant materials, despite my careful identification and collection? Incorrect preparation methods, despite following historical recipes with obsessive precision? Some kind of individual physiological resistance that made Remmy immune to compounds that should have been universally toxic?

Or worse—had some part of me been consistently sabotaging my own efforts, measuring incorrectly without conscious awareness, diluting preparations through subconscious moral resistance to what I was attempting to accomplish?

The possibility that my own psychology was protecting Remmy from my conscious intentions was almost more disturbing than outright failure would have been. It suggested that even when I'd committed fully to murder, some deeper part of my mind was rebelling against the action, undermining my own plans.

What kind of killer was consistently thwarted by her own conscience? What kind of murderer was too fundamentally decent to succeed at her chosen profession, even when success would solve problems that seemed unsolvable through any other method?

Without another sound, I eased out from under the covers, my movements careful and deliberate. The plush carpet muffled my steps as I slipped into the bathroom and closed the door with a soft click.

Then the sickness hit me like a tsunami of physical and psychological revulsion.

I gripped the edge of the marble sink, but my knees buckled anyway, forcing me down to the cold tile floor beside the toilet. My stomach seized in violent rebellion against everything I'd consumed, thought, and attempted in the past twenty-four hours.

The champagne came up first, then the wedding cake that had tasted like sawdust in my mouth, then the carefully orchestrated dinner I'd barely managed to swallow while monitoring Remmy.

When the retching finally stopped, I stayed kneeling on the bathroom floor, my forehead pressed against the porcelain while my body shook with tremors.

This was the physical manifestation of complete moral bankruptcy combined with absolute practical failure. I'd spent months researching methods of killing while maintaining the facade of wedding planning and domestic contentment.

All that corruption—and I still couldn't even manage to kill the man who trusted me most.

The knowledge sat in my chest like a malignant tumor—impossible to remove, certain to spread. It didn't matter that I'd failed; the intent alone had rewritten my DNA. Whatever I was before, I wasn't innocent anymore.

When I walked back into the bedroom, Remmy was sitting up against the pillows, looking refreshed and energetic in ways that should have been medically impossible. His eyes were clear and bright, his color excellent.

"That tea knocked me out—" he paused, frowning like he almost remembered something, "—completely."

There was something else in his phrasing that caught my attention and made my skin crawl. He sounded almost... proud of the tea's effectiveness, as if my herbal blend had exceeded his expectations in ways that gave him particular satisfaction. Not just grateful for good sleep, but pleased with the specific results of consuming something I'd prepared with his death in mind.

"What were you doing in there?" he asked, nodding toward the bathroom where I'd just finished vomiting up my guilt and disappointment and rage.

"Washing up," I said automatically.

He smiled with the ease of someone who'd never had to hide secrets that could destroy lives, someone whose biggest deceptions involved surprise gifts and birthday party planning rather than systematic attempts at spousal murder.

"Hey, but really, thanks for that tea last night," he continued, bouncing slightly on the mattress. "I feel incredible today. Better than I have in weeks. What did you put in it exactly?"

My mouth went dry. "Just... chamomile, mostly. And some valerian root for deeper sleep. Nothing you haven't had before."

Nothing except the carefully concentrated extracts of toxic roots, measured with pharmaceutical precision and administered with the intent of stopping his heart before dawn broke over our honeymoon suite.

"Well, whatever the exact combination was, it worked like magic," he said, stretching his arms above his head with obvious satisfaction and vitality. "I feel like I could run a marathon. You should seriously consider bottling that stuff—people would pay premium prices for sleep that effective and restorative."

The suggestion was innocent, even playful, but it landed in my consciousness like mockery. Here was my now husband, alive and energetic and grateful for the poison I'd failed to administer properly, suggesting that I commercialize my murder attempts as luxury sleep aids for an upscale market demographic.

The cosmic irony was almost too perfect to bear. I'd spent months perfecting what I believed were lethal formulations, only to discover that my expertise lay in creating the world's most effective wellness products.

"I should get ready," I said, unable to tolerate another moment of his unconscious taunting. "People will be expecting updates about how the wedding went, and I need to start on thank-you notes while the details are still fresh in everyone's memory."

"Don't work too hard on all that social obligation stuff," he said, pulling me down for a kiss that tasted like toothpaste and trust. "We've got our whole lives ahead of us to handle the administrative side of being married."

*Our whole lives.* The phrase should have filled me with anticipation or at least contentment—the promise of decades together, building something permanent and meaningful through shared experience and mutual devotion. Growing old side by side while accumulating the kind of deep intimacy that only comes from choosing the same person every day for years at a time.

Instead, it felt like a prison sentence. I was married to someone who had no idea he was condemning me to spend the rest of my existence carrying the knowledge of what I'd tried to do to him, what I was apparently still planning to do to him, and what kind of person I'd discovered myself to be when pushed beyond the boundaries of conventional problem-solving approaches.

How was I supposed to spend a lifetime with someone I'd repeatedly tried to kill? How could I accept his love, his trust, his assumptions about shared future when I'd proven that my commitment to our marriage extended only as far as my ability to tolerate being controlled by his vision of what our life together should look like?

The knowledge would poison every interaction from now forward. I would spend the rest of our marriage knowing exactly what I was capable of planning and attempting, while he remained blissfully oblivious to how many times he'd come close to dying at the hands of someone who was supposed to love him unconditionally.

But as I rode the elevator down to the lobby, studying my reflection in the mirrored walls—perfect posture, controlled expression, the appearance of someone who could blend into any social situation and maintain any necessary performance—I realized that my repeated failures had taught me something valuable about myself.

I wasn't done trying. The disappointment I felt wasn't moral revulsion at what I'd attempted, but professional frustration at my inability to execute plans that should have been straightforward.

I'd failed multiple times, but failure was educational. I'd learned what didn't work—and that was enough to keep me trying. I could refine my methods, improve my precision, and make the next attempt cleaner.

Next time—and there would be a next time—I'd be smarter. More careful. More patient.

The elevator doors opened onto the hotel lobby, the world unchanged while I was not.

The question wasn't whether I'd try again, but when I'd find out what I'd missed.

Either way, I was no longer the same woman who'd entered this hotel as a nervous bride. I was someone who understood her purpose now—and purpose, once discovered, doesn't die easily.

I could hear the buzz of my own thoughts as I tried to motion through a seemingly normal day.

In the reflection of the glass doors, a man was watching me—calm, patient, familiar. When I turned, no one was there.

# Chapter 18:

# Cousins

By the time I walked into the lobby, I'd settled my face into the right shape—open, recently married, a little tired in a way that read as charming. I'd been adjusting that face all morning in the mirror, smoothing the corners like fresh plaster, making sure nothing underneath bled through.

In the mirrored panel above the elevator buttons, I had practiced the smile twice, then let it fall the moment the doors opened, like peeling off damp clothes. Weddings teach you to smile on command. I'd learned to make it believable.

The cousins spotted me first. They were already near the revolving doors with to-go coffees and a level of energy I didn't trust before noon.

"Emily!" one of them chirped, bright as the logos stamped on their shopping totes. This was Ava—sharp jaw, high ponytail, the one who narrated life like she expected a camera to be following. Her sister, Brooke, smiled more quietly, the softer twin if you squinted, although they weren't twins at all. Brooke had the kind of face people confessed to and then regretted it later.

They hugged me like we were closer than we were. Their brightness felt like being handed a vase I hadn't asked for.

"How's the Mrs. this morning?" Ava asked, a little wink tucked inside the sentence.

"Functional," I said, letting the word do everything—honest, breezy, done.

"It's the day after," Brooke said, gentle. "You don't have to be on."

They meant it. And I liked them for it. Which annoyed me. Kindness always made me feel like I was being inspected for cracks.

We slid into a black SUV that Remmy had arranged, which made us feel important for exactly five seconds. The driver asked for a destination and the cousins negotiated a rough circuit—boutiques, lunch, a place Ava swore had "dangerously good" lemon bars.

When the car pulled away from the curb, I let my head tilt against the cool window and watched the hotel facade shrink behind us.

We passed the bar on the corner and noticed Matt with a mug between his hands. Tea, or coffee pretending to be. He glanced up as if he felt eyes on him, but the SUV had already merged into traffic.

"You've been to Mercer & Pine?" Ava's voice floated back to me, already on to scarves and handbags.

"I've walked by," I said, which wasn't a lie. "I liked the window."

"We'll fix that," she said. "Brooke loves a mission."

"I love a discount," Brooke corrected, and we all laughed, a low ribbon of sound looping the car into something like ease.

The city wore its late morning well—gold light, storefronts yawning awake, pedestrians focused on their own tasks. The city pretended it wasn't watching, and I pretended not to notice.

"You're classic," Brooke said, pinning a scarf on me when we entered the first shop. "You like things that looks like they never tried."

"She's stealth," Ava said. "I respect that."

I let them talk about me like a silhouette. It was easier than offering content. My job was to be the negative space in their portrait—present enough to complete it, but not enough to distract.

At the third store, a rack of linen dresses skated on a track and the air smelled like cedar and money. Ava lifted a dress that looked like clouds had learned structure. "You could wear this anywhere."

Anywhere. I thought of last night's tea, the way steam curled from the mug like a benediction, the glass vial empty and gleaming. I thought of this morning's stillness and how it had felt curated, like the world

250

trying to hand me a frame. In that frame, Remmy's breath had been the one thing out of place.

I tried the dress. It made me look like a promise I couldn't keep.

The dress was a costume for a character I didn't want to play.

The mirror showed me performing normal. I could almost believe it if I didn't blink.

"You okay?" Brooke asked as I stepped down from the mirror platform, her voice a soft nudge. "You keep zoning out and then apologizing without saying anything out loud." She smiled. "It's impressive."

People always ask if you're okay, in the exact tone that makes you feel like you're not.

"I didn't sleep much," I said. "Wedding hangover."

Ava bumped my shoulder with hers. "You still look disgustingly good."

That was the trick: convince the world that your ruin lived under a perfect coat of paint. My mother taught me that, though she never called it teaching. More like correction. It was a trick I learned young—let them think they've seen under the surface, but never show them the foundation.

Make sure everything is in its place.

I heard her every time I adjusted a hem.

At lunch, the cousins ordered sparkling water without looking at the menu. I asked for the same, holding the glass up to the light and watching the bubbles race themselves to death.

"So," Ava said, sliding sunglasses to the top of her head. "We never got the gossip. The DJ drama? Matt said something and then said he wasn't supposed to say something and it was very, like, theater-kid coy."

My stomach tightened. "What did he say?"

"That Chuck had a falling out with the DJ, that he told you he wouldn't play." Ava stabbed her salad with cheerful violence. "There was some last-minute switch, and Remmy took a bullet on it."

A bullet. The word flashed hot. I pictured the entry wound, neat and almost polite, and wondered if that was what she thought had been done for me. "A bullet how?"

"Well, you know Chuck," Brooke whispered. "He doesn't want people to know he has money trouble. That's why he made Remmy reach out to Thomas." She took a bite, sitting back. "Totally fucked up, if you ask me."

Ava waved her fork. "You're so bad. It's not our business." She looked at me sympathetically. "You got the DJ, so Remmy must have worked it out, right?"

I blinked. "I didn't know about any of this."

They exchanged a look, realizing they shared too much.

Brooke leaned in a little. "Remmy's family has been under a pile. Medical bills that spiraled, then Chuck's retirement stocks haven't been performing, and he was too proud to ask for help. Remmy's been covering where he can. He called in favors for the wedding, is the point. I think something happened with the DJ and the final bill, and it blew out of proportion."

The world rearranged itself by a millimeter. Not enough to fix anything. Enough to make me hate them for the attempt.

"Remmy should have told me," I said. I kept my tone mild, tucked into the linen napkin.

"Totally," Ava said, sympathetic like a teacher. "Something about all the males in the Black family. They think protecting people means doing it quietly and dumb."

Brooke nodded. "He's not... secretive. He's... absorbent. And then he leaks at the worst time." That was the trouble with men like him—they believed in fixing the leak while ignoring the rot in the beams.

I made myself smile. "That sounds right."

They turned the conversation to a cousin who'd decided to raise chickens on a balcony. I let the words pass like a river around a stone.

I sipped my water and imagined breaking the straw between my fingers.

We shared lemon bars at the place Ava swore by. She was right; they were incredible. Powdered sugar dusted my fingertips as if a crime scene. It felt almost dangerous, to enjoy something so small when my questions were still unresolved.

Pleasure was a muscle—flex it too easily, and it might forget the work it was meant for.

For a few minutes, I let the practical sweets blunt the edges inside me.

"You know," Brooke said, dabbing her mouth with a napkin, "I always thought Remmy would marry someone like... I don't know. Someone simple."

Ava winced. "Brooke."

"No, I mean it as a compliment." She looked at me. "You're not simple. You see all the way around something and then decide anyway."

It landed like an accusation dressed as praise. Sometimes the truest things sound like insults that forgot their tone.

But it also made something inside me settle. Someone had named me correctly in a sentence without knowing what it cost.

The afternoon stretched. We drifted in and out of shops like we were rehearsing a life. At one, Ava tried on sunglasses and did impressions of everyone in the family. At another, Brooke bought a gift for a niece with a note that would make the girl feel like the only person on earth.

They were good at this—being people. Standing next to them felt like standing next to a well—deep, full, and utterly uninterested in your thirst. Almost unbearable to stand near.

We were halfway back to the SUV when Brooke slowed. "You like him," she said. Not a question. She didn't say Remmy's name because she didn't need to. "In the real way."

"I married him," I said.

"People marry for worse reasons than the right one," she said. "I'm sorry about the morning."

I kept my face smooth. "What about it?"

Brooke tucked her hair behind her ear. "You looked like someone who woke up inside a different story than the one she rehearsed."

Ava whistled low. "Jesus, Brookie. You're not allowed to psychoanalyze the bride. Give her a week."

"I'm fine," I said, and made it sound like a fact the world would be foolish to question.

They let it go. The kindness of that made me want to bite.

Back in the SUV, I watched the city's light shift into an evening glow, every glass surface turned to a mirror trying to catch us. I watched our reflection over and over—three women pretending the day belonged to them.

It should have meant something. I had wanted today to be the first chapter of the pity I had earned, the visible kind, the kind that lives in casseroles and people lowering their voices when they say your name.

I had curated a life that could hold it: the lawn without weeds, the house with lines, the friends who believed they knew me, the spreadsheets without debt. The surface gleaming enough to make the crack in the center look like art.

My mother had taught me the necessity of surface. She'd also taught me the price of failing it.

She called it discipline. I called it the reason I could keep a straight face while the ground moved.

Girls like me learned to sacrifice early and without applause. People like Remmy believed in a world that caught them, every time.

I told myself this wasn't about cruelty. It was about balance. The pruning that kept the whole hedge healthy. Remove one branch. Save the shape.

Some people believe in safety nets—others believe in sharp edges. We'd both chosen our faith long ago.

I believed I was a good person. I believed that even as I placed him on the altar of narrative and sharpened the knife of my intention. I believed it because the alternative required a different word I wasn't ready to wear.

By the time the SUV pulled into the hotel's block, the cousins were promising dinner at some point soon, maybe a spa day, maybe a Sunday hike that everyone would cancel and then reschedule. I believed they meant it. I believed they liked me. And for a brief, treacherous second, I wondered if there was still a version of the story where I didn't go through with any of the planning at all.

Even wondering about another version of the story felt like a betrayal of the one I'd rehearsed.

If this was my life now—if the plan had to wait— maybe I could make the most of its arrangement. I could stand inside it and smile and say thank you at the right volume.

But stories don't wait for your edits.

Ava squeezed my hand as the car slowed. "You did good, Mrs. B." The words landed like a period on a sentence I hadn't finished writing.

The first thing I saw wasn't the uniforms or the faces—it was the light. Blue and red, folding over itself in slow, relentless pulses, painting the trees and the sidewalk like a warning in two colors.

The color drained from the day, leaving only the pulse of sirens.

The air had the static edge of an oncoming storm, and for a second I couldn't hear my own breath over the dull throb of the engines idling at the curb.

# Chapter 19:

# Ambulance

The SUV slowed and the driver swore softly under his breath, the sound too polite to register. People clogged the sidewalk in the way they do when they're deciding whether a story belongs to them.

For a moment, I thought about how easily crowds give themselves permission to stand close to a stranger's pain. It's a kind of trespass they'll never admit to. In their eyes, the scene was already theirs—a story they could tell over dinner, embellishing the details until the truth was unrecognizable.

"What the..." Ava's voice stretched thin. "Is that our hotel?"

The driver braked. We were still a block away, but the barricades already stitched the street closed, yellow tape catching the light like a row of small suns. The air smelled faintly of diesel from the generator, thick enough that it sat on my tongue.

Somewhere behind the crowd, someone laughed a shade too brightly, the kind of laugh people use when they realize this isn't their tragedy.

The thrum of radios layered over the hum of engines. I felt the migraine arrive without asking permission, a pressure blooming at the hinge of my jaw and behind my eyes.

"Do you want me to try around the block?" the driver asked.

"Please," Brooke said, her voice trying to be soothing.

We looped the block, then another. Every approach offered a different angle on the same refusal. Police stood in a posture you only learn from standing like that a long time—weight in one hip, eyes scanning with boredom that was mostly a mask for vigilance, the stance of men who had memorized their own shadows. Guests gathered in clumps.

One man kept pointing toward the building as if rehearsing a news interview, pausing every so often to adjust his stance.

A woman wept on the curb in the theatrical way of people who need strangers to know they feel things deeply. A bellhop smoked with the intensity of someone who had been told not to.

We parked a block over and walked. The air had shifted into the evening's metallic cool. Sneakers and heels and dress shoes made a composite rhythm on the cracked sidewalk. The cousins kept close to me without making it obvious; I loved and hated them in the same breath for that.

The warmth of their nearness was almost unbearable—like someone holding a match too close to the skin. It reminded me of hospital waiting rooms and holiday tables, of all the places where kindness feels like an interrogation you can't step away from.

At the first barricade, an officer held up a hand. "Sorry, folks, we need this area clear."

"We're guests," Ava said, because Ava always had the paperwork ready in her pocket even if it was imaginary. "Is there a fire? A gas leak? What happened?"

"Ma'am, I can't say," the officer said. His eyes flicked to me like they would to a bruise you're pretending isn't there. If I had let my mouth tremble, he would have softened by a degree.

Brooke tried the other flank. "Is there a way in on Ninth?"

He shook his head. "We'll make an announcement when we can."

We drifted away because there was nowhere else to put our bodies. People flowed around us in small currents. Somewhere, a radio crackled with a series of numbers that meant more to men with clipped haircuts than to anyone who loved a person inside a building.

"Okay," Ava said in the voice of women who build plans out of thin air. "We wait. We text. We don't panic because that's a waste of salt."

It would have been easy—too easy—to think of the tea. To call up the image of his hand around the mug, the way his eyelids softened last night, the heaviness that slid into his voice before he folded into bed.

Was this the slow curve of it, the delayed arc? Had I miscounted my calculations? I pictured the scene as if it belonged to someone else: a man collapsing under chandeliers, the cup from the night before still in his system like a time-delayed confession. It could have been elegant, cinematic even—if only I could claim it.

Had the story delivered me a perfect scene and I'd failed to recognize it?

I pressed my teeth together until my jaw hurt and looked at the tape again.

It took an hour for the story to leak in the way stories do when they have to jump barricades. Snippets first, then a name that traveled from mouth to mouth with the sticky speed of rumor. The cousins' phones buzzed and stilled and then buzzed again. One of them gasped at the text and covered her mouth with her hand like she could push the sound back in.

Time folded in on itself—every voice around us dropped to a muffled hum. Brooke's eyes found mine, wide and wet, and I knew whatever was about to cross her lips would rearrange the air. My pulse stuttered.

"Emily," Brooke said softly, her face wrong in a way that made something animal in me need to sit, even though there was nowhere to go. "There was an incident. They're saying..."

The world did a small tilt. "Say it," I said, and my voice was an obedient thing.

"Remmy," she whispered, like you speak in a church whether you believe in God or not. "They went to his room... Paramedics—he didn't—"

She didn't finish. She didn't have to. The word lived in the space after her sentence like a shadow that would not move.

It came uninvited—a thin, electric flicker under my ribs. Not joy. Not exactly. It was the shadow of something I didn't have a name for—a recognition, maybe, that the script could be rewritten without my hand on the pen. I smothered it like a flame under glass, willing it to disappear before it left smoke.

My knees softened, my breath hitched, my hand flew to my mouth in a gesture I had practiced as a child in the mirror, testing what grief would look like on a face that was supposed to be stoic.

I angled my face toward the tape, knowing the light would catch the wet in my eyes just enough. I let my bottom lip tremble for half a second before pressing it flat again. Too much would read as theatrical; just enough would be remembered.

"No," I said, the vowel catching. "No, that's—are you sure?" I turned my head as if the answer could be different if I gave the light a different angle of my cheekbone. "He was—this morning he was—"

Ava's arms were around me and then Brooke's, and a stranger handed me a water bottle that I didn't take. The cousins made a small wall with their bodies the way women do.

I let my weight find theirs. I let my shoulders shake at a volume that signaled ladylike devastation. My mother would have approved—grief restrained, controlled, never spilling into the kind of mess that stains upholstery.

I did not wail. I did not go still. I chose the middle place, the one that people remember as dignified.

Sirens swelled close and then far and then close again. Someone shouted. A radio hissed. A man argued with an officer about access because rules are suggestions meant for other people. The tape fluttered, a bright line between before and after.

I stared at the hotel and thought of how quiet the suite had been this morning.

The silence had been its own kind of gift, the sort you don't open in front of others. I'd walked through it like a gallery, touching nothing, letting my eyes linger on the empty spaces where his presence should have been. Now, that same absence pressed against me from across the street, louder than the sirens.

Behind my eyes, a reel clicked through possibilities. If I had not killed him and he was dead, someone else had. Or nothing had. Bodies quit; that was their only promise. Maybe he had been carrying the wrong weight for too long—other people's debts, other people's calm. Maybe the bullet he took to fix my evening had been the wrong kind of bullet.

"Yes?" I heard a woman shout nearby. "I'm his mom."

But when I turned, I didn't see Marlene. I saw the resemblance of someone I had known—someone familiar I couldn't place.

The police officer was talking to the woman, her body collapsing into them as they spoke. As they gently lowered her to the ground to seat her, a flicker of recognition flashed.

Laura Kowalski. Matt's mom.

My brain stalled—how could she be here?

"Do we call her?" Brooke asked, careful, because Brooke had seen something in me I didn't want anyone to see and still chose to speak to me like I was worth choosing.

"She'll hear," Ava said. They meant Remmy's mother. But my mind was already elsewhere.

The conversation rang in my ears like an echo in a fishbowl. *Remmy is dead. Matt's mom is here. Matt is... dead?*

Ava squeezed my hand. "We've got you."

I made the appropriate nod. I forced a tear to fall and didn't swipe it away. In the lights, it felt staged in the correct way. People would tell this story later—how the bride stood behind the tape on the day after, how she pressed her hands together and stared at the doors like a saint, a soldier, and something else.

Then someone said my name with official weight, and the world came back into its edges.

"Mrs. Black?"

I turned toward the voice and rearranged my face one more time.

"Yes," I said, looking up at an officer in full uniform.

Somewhere ahead of me, a life was already taking shape, with or without my permission.

# Chapter 20:

# The End

Remmy Black and Matt Kowalski were found side by side, both deceased with no visible wounds. No fingerprints that didn't belong, no hair out of place. Both were found in a vacant room on the second floor.

By the time the headlines reached me, the story had already begun to write itself.

I'd rehearsed this scene for months without knowing it—every tilt of the head, every swallow timed to grief instead of guilt.

Detective Rodriguez was assigned to the case, bringing me into the station. I knew to call a lawyer, though I knew even better to give it a beat before.

Much less practiced. Much more like a grieving widow.

"The initial results demonstrate a heart attack. I'm not sure what I can explain." I wiped my waterline, brushing the tissue against my eye to form a tear.

"Two heart attacks simultaneously? Not only your husband, but his best friend." The detective's eyes lowered. "How does that happen?"

My eye contact held. "Sir, respectfully, I can't explain something I wasn't there for. I have numerous witnesses, including my husband's family, who were with me the entire day."

The officer held eye contact, unflinching.

"Remmy had been having cardiovascular problems. He had been seeing a doctor, a specialist, even." A cold clarity spread through me—the realization that I was getting away with it.

His tests showed strain. I dabbed a tear at the right moment.

"As for Matt, I can't speak to him. He's Remmy's best friend, and Remmy is my husband." I straightened my spine. "Now, are you going to continue grilling a widow, or am I going to contact every press publication in the nation to share the story of the widow who was held against her will after losing her husband on her wedding night?"

By the time they let me go, I'd already rewritten the narrative in their notebooks.

I found Ms. Volkova in her garden three hours after Detective Rodriguez had finished grilling me on Remmy and Matt's deaths, though it was clear off the bat they had nothing to go off.

She was deadheading roses with the same methodical precision she brought to everything.

The afternoon sun cast long shadows across her yard, and in that golden light, her garden looked less like hobby horticulture and more like a carefully curated collection of specimens. I'd walked through this space dozens of times over the past months, admiring the beauty without fully appreciating the sophistication of what she'd assembled.

Now, with questions about plant toxicology consuming my thoughts, I saw her garden differently. This wasn't a hobby—it was a laboratory disguised as landscaping.

"I heard about Remmy," she said without looking up from her work, her voice carrying the appropriate note of sympathy while her hands continued their systematic removal of dying petals. "Such a shock for someone so young and healthy. You must be devastated."

The word choice was precise, clinical. Not heartbroken or shattered or any of the other emotional descriptors that people typically used when discussing sudden loss.

"I don't understand what happened," I said, moving behind the stone bench she'd positioned near her prize-winning delphiniums. "He seemed so healthy yesterday, so full of energy. The doctors are saying heart failure, but he never had any symptoms, any warning signs."

We both knew I was lying.

Ms. Volkova's pruning shears paused for just a moment—barely perceptible, but I'd learned to notice details that other people missed. "Sometimes the heart simply stops," she said carefully. "Especially when it's been under stress that isn't immediately apparent. Wedding planning, changes in routine, disrupted sleep patterns. The cardiovascular system can be more fragile than we realize."

Her explanation was medically plausible, the kind of information that would comfort most grieving widows by providing rational explanations for inexplicable loss.

But in this moment, she wasn't attempting to comfort me—she was attempting to provide details to a story I was still crafting.

My fingers swirled the familiar bench between us, questions circling my mind like a hawk.

"I didn't do anything different..." My voice trailed off at the end. I was testing her response to see how much she actually knew or participated in. To get down to the answers of the delayed dose, of Matt—of all of it.

"How... the delay... Matt..." the words were coming out all at once. "You know a great deal about herbal preparations. What do you know?"

She paused, tossing her shears into a pile of mud. "I know enough to know you left too many clues."

Ice seized my veins.

"I've studied traditional plant medicine for many years. My grandmother was what people used to call a wise woman—someone who understood that nature provides remedies for many conditions, if you know where to look and how to prepare them properly." Ms. Volkova's voice took on a reminiscent quality, as if she was remembering lessons learned decades ago. "Do you remember the lesson I taught you?"

My eyes scanned hers, searching for an answer.

"The petals were falling apart," she said, firmer this time.

I felt the words tightening around my throat. "What do you mean?"

Volkova leaned closer to me, her gloved hands resting on the stone as if it were a pew between us. "You think I didn't see the way your hand shook at the table? You grew careless. Sloppy." Her eyes flicked past me toward the house. "So I corrected it."

The word landed like a diagnosis, not an insult.

My stomach lurched. "Corrected—"

"I didn't switch the mixture." Her tone was matter-of-fact, as though she were explaining the proper way to prune a rose. "I simply... added compounds to delay it. Your mix was too strong, too bitter. He would have noticed, and then all your careful rehearsing would have been wasted."

Heat prickled behind my ears. "You—"

"Women like us do what we do only when we get it right," she cut in, her voice lowering to a hiss. "And someone was already listening.

I knew who she meant before she said his name.

The world tilted, the ground uncertain beneath me. "Matt?"

"Matt," she confirmed. Her eyes narrowed. "He was always watching. Always closer than you think. And you, child, you gave him enough to feed on."

The garden fell silent except for the pulse in my ears, the air thick with the scent of cut stems and damp earth. Volkova turned back to her shears as if nothing monumental had just been spoken, her voice returning to its soft, instructive cadence.

"Everything blooms when it's ready. Force it, and the petals fall apart faster," she repeated behind her gritted teeth.

The garden was damp, the soil clinging to my shoes as if the earth wanted to hold me in place. Volkova's words had a sharp message—*I did you a favor.*

I should have hated her for it. She changed my carefully orchestrated plan, stole the moment I had rehearsed in my mind a thousand times. And yet, as the condolences piled up on my doorstep, as neighbors whispered my name in hushed tones, as casseroles and pity arrived in equal measure, I felt the crown settle anyway. Widow. Revered. Untouchable.

And still—empty.

***

One evening, weeks later, I stood at the fence, fingers tracing the iron bars like confession beads. The gratitude slipped out in a whisper, fragile and unfinished. "Thank you. For... what you did."

Volkova tilted her head, her eyes unreadable, her clippers glinting in the last of the daylight. "You're welcome, child. You got what you wanted."

I swallowed. My voice dropped lower, sheepish, betraying more than I meant to. "But I didn't get to do it my way. Not the way I planned."

The silence between us stretched, heavy as soil before bloom.

"How long have you been watching me?" The question escaped before I could stop it.

Volkova's smile was slow, deliberate. "Since the day you moved in. Some flowers announce themselves immediately." She set down her clippers, giving me her full attention for the first time. "You carried yourself like someone who understood that beauty requires sacrifice. I simply waited to see what you would be willing to cut away."

"And Matt?"

"Matt was a weed," she said simply. "Growing too close, threatening the garden's design. He would have choked out everything we planted." Her eyes glinted in the fading light. "Two birds, one stone. Efficient."

I felt the weight of her planning, how I'd been both student and instrument. "You orchestrated everything."

"I guided. You chose." She picked up her shears again, testing the blade against her thumb. "Every dose you administered, every mixture you prepared—those were your decisions. I merely... refined the timing." She snipped her shears once, sharp. "Matt was for you, but also for me."

The distinction felt important to her, this separation between influence and action. I wondered if it helped her sleep at night, or if sleep came as easily to her as it had stopped coming to me.

"The delayed reaction," I pressed. "How did you—"

"Chemistry, child." And she left it at that. She gestured toward the house where Remmy used to sit, dreaming of our future together.

I thought of him lifting that champagne glass, the way he'd smiled at me over the rim. How trusting he'd been, even at the end.

"And now?" I asked.

Volkova studied me with the same intensity she brought to her prize specimens. "Now you understand what you are. What you've always been." She paused, examining me. "Most people spend their entire lives pretending they're not predators. You have the honesty to embrace it."

The word—*predator*—should have stung. Instead, it settled over me like a coat that finally fit properly.

"Some weeds require more than pruning."

I understood then that this wasn't about Remmy specifically. It was about a larger garden, one that stretched far beyond our suburban neighborhood.

"You'll teach me," I said. Not a question.

"I'll guide," she corrected. "The rest will be your choice. Always your choice."

The air seemed to shift, the night blooming wider around her words. A shiver slid down my spine, half fear, half recognition. This was my inheritance—not Remmy's life insurance or the house we'd barely had time to make into a home, but this knowledge, this capability, this terrible clarity about what needed to be done.

I pressed my hand flat against the fence, feeling the cold iron root me where I stood. The widow's crown still rested on my head, invisible but unmistakable. I'd earned it through failure and it had been perfected by someone who understood the long game.

"When do we start?" I asked.

Volkova's smile was sharp as her garden shears. "We already have."

She turned back to her roses, dismissing me with the same casual authority she'd shown from the beginning. But as I walked back toward the house—my house now, mine alone—I heard her voice carry across the cooling air.

"Same time tomorrow, Emily. Bring a notebook. Real learning requires documentation."

At the door, I looked back at her silhouette, the knot in my chest loosening. I hadn't lost the moment, only the chance to make it mine.

The garden would bloom again.

# Bound in Botany

*Book Two of the Root & Vein Trilogy*

# Bound in Botany Chapter 1
## (Rooted in Silence Sequel)

The rain wasn't hard enough to keep anyone away—just steady enough to make the grass slick and the air smell like wet stone. It clung to my shoes in beads, unable to decide whether to fall or hold fast, the way some part of me still couldn't decide whether to believe what I'd been told on Saturday.

The officer had stood in my doorway like he'd practiced it in front of a mirror: cap in his hands, voice sanded flat. He said *suicide pact*, like it was a phrase that belonged in ordinary vocabulary, like my brother and his best friend had just shaken hands on oblivion. I'd nodded, but inside, something else had locked into place.

Not grief first. Not shock. A cold click in my chest.

Matt did not do this to himself.

But I was the only one carrying that certainty through the rows of umbrellas this morning, and the certainty felt heavy.

Nelson's palm rested on my shoulder, steady, guiding, like we were in a play and he'd memorized the blocking. He squeezed at the right moments—the priest's pauses, the muffled sobs from the crowd—and I hated him for being so competent at it.

What he couldn't know was that grief wasn't what I carried. It was a sharpened resistance, an insistence that everyone else was wrong.

We stood among strangers who claimed Matt's legacy in cheap words—the guy with the big laugh, the firefighter who'd risk anything.

None of them could summon that laugh, not really. Their mouths twisted the memory like it was borrowed. The priest's voice cracked as he tried to turn Matt into scripture, his breath fogging in the damp air.

Matt would've hated this. All the order, all the solemnity. He would've wanted beer cracked open in the parking lot, greasy pizza boxes, stories so raw they hurt from laughing. He would've heckled the priest just to remind everyone that reverence was a waste of time.

But my mother wasn't here to say it. She hadn't made it out of bed since Saturday.

The officer had come to my door after breaking the news to her—asked her to come to the hotel, to sit across from men in pressed uniforms who explained how her son had chosen to die.

She came home and never came out again. The shades stayed drawn, the house silent except for the sound of her pacing from one end of the hall to the other.

And when the funeral came, the cousins whispered excuses. "She's not ready." "She's too fragile."

But I knew the truth. My mother was already buried. Not with Matt, not yet, but under the weight of a story she accepted without a fight.

That was the difference.

She curled inward.

I sharpened outward.

Instead of a kegger, Matt got lilies. Black umbrellas. A casket lowered with military precision.

Matthew James Kowalski: Firefighter. Son. Friend.

The straps whined, the ground yawned, and everyone shifted forward for their chance to perform grief. Toss a flower. Cross yourself. Say something safe.

The sound of earth hitting wood went through me like a key turning in a lock.

And that's when I saw her.

She stood ten feet back, trying to vanish in plain sight. Black hat pulled too low, sunglasses too wide, jacket zipped up like armor. The disguise wasn't for warmth—it was for control. A woman who knew how cameras worked, who knew how to stage a moment.

Emily Black.

The papers had already renamed her: *From Byrd to Black: The Widow's Nightmare.* Today, she looked smaller, tighter, as if holding herself in so nothing leaked out. She held no rose, offered no prayer. She just... watched.

Our eyes caught. Five seconds? Six? Long enough for something to pass between us that wasn't rain or grief. Then the crowd shifted, umbrellas swayed, and she was gone in the noise.

Nelson leaned in, breath coffee-sour under the mint. "Do you want to go?"

I shook my head. "Not yet."

Because I wanted to see who lingered. Who looked twice. Who couldn't stop themselves.

When the crowd thinned, she was still there, near the sycamore at the edge of the plot. Not hidden. Not bold. Half-turned, like she was listening for something beneath the soil.

And beside her—shorter, older, dark glasses, still as a shadow—A woman I didn't know then.

Later, I would.

Someone coughed, hacking into the silence, and the moment snapped. By the time I blinked, she was gone. Or she wanted me to think she was.

The gravediggers returned, their shovels cutting into mud, the rhythm of the dirt piling in time with the rain. People muttered prayers, relief disguised as reverence. Action is comfort when words won't hold.

I stood until the casket was fully covered, until the last flower sank into the mud. My toes were numb, my coat heavy.

Nelson tugged at me, urging me toward the car. I let him lead, my body moving while my eyes stayed back on the grave, on the sycamore, on the empty patch where Emily had been.

Inside the car, the heater whirred too hot, fogging the windshield until Nelson cracked his window. He drove slow through the cemetery's narrow roads, the names on the stones blurring past.

"You okay?" he asked finally. His voice was careful, like stepping onto a frozen pond.

"I think so," I said. "It's weird."

"You don't have to know yet." His hand found mine on the seat between us, squeezing. A script again.

I turned to the window. The glass was streaked with water, and beyond it, names carved into stone slid by. Each one was a story already shut.

Matt's wasn't. Not yet.

"Hungry?" Nelson asked.

"Serrato's is close," I said. "Or we could stop at my dad's."

He hesitated. "Are you sure that's a good idea? Seeing him now?"

"He's still alive. Avoiding him won't change that."

"Sometimes..." he clicked his tongue, a sound that always meant he thought he was wise, "sometimes it's easier to let go early. Before it gets worse."

The knot in my stomach tightened.

My father had been unraveling for years— schizophrenia gnawing at him until reality was just scraps. He'd shouted at cupboards to scare off ghosts, patched leaks with duct tape, held conversations with people who weren't there.

When my mother finally left, she took us, and our lives lightened instantly. But still, he'd never stopped trying. Never stopped being my dad, even when his mind betrayed him.

Nelson thought the nicest thing he left behind was a lawn that didn't need mowing. That was how he summarized a man's life—like folding an obituary into a fortune cookie. Neat. Useless.

I wanted to say, *You're wrong.* I wanted to tell him about the way my father fixed a chair just to prove it could be done, the way he stretched every dollar until it screamed, the way he loved us in whatever fragments he had left.

But Nelson would only nod politely, wait for me to run out of air, then move on.

So I nodded instead. Let him think he was right.

He squeezed my hand again. "We should get a trust going. For when we have kids." The way he said *kids* was casual, like they were already in the backseat waiting for their turn.

The thought made my stomach flip.

"Actually," I said, pulling my hand away, "I'm not feeling great. Let's order delivery."

"Sure, honey. Want me to grab ginger ale?"

"No. Just home."

He nodded, easy as always, and drove on.

That was what made it hard. It would've been easier if he were cruel.

Instead, he was the man who brought me soup when I couldn't keep water down, the man who texted Matt behind my back just to make sure I was okay. He'd shown up when no one else did.

But he'd also never had a police officer stand in the doorway with his cap in his hands, telling him how his brother chose his own death. He hadn't heard the word *suicide* and felt the lock click in his chest.

That was mine alone.

When we reached home, I told him I needed to lie down. He kissed my forehead, murmured something comforting, and went to the garage to work on whatever men like him needed to keep their hands busy.

I shut myself in the bedroom, pulled one of Matt's old sweatshirts over my head, and lay on top of the covers, eyes fixated on the ceiling.

I replayed the five-second stare with Emily until it expanded into minutes... hours. Until I could feel the weight of her gaze pressed against mine, steady, deliberate.

I thought of the woman beside her—short, sharp, half-hidden. A shadow with a face.

The way dark eyes haunted me, focused and poisonous, even behind her dark-lensed sunglasses.

I thought of Matt's laugh, the one none of them could replicate. The one they buried with him.

The house was silent, but I could still hear the scrape of shovels, the thud of dirt, the lock in my chest clicking into place.

They would all move on. Say prayers, eat casseroles, file paperwork.

But I wasn't done.

Not yet.

Not with Emily.

Not with the story.

Not with the truth.

# Acknowledgements

To my husband, Ryan—my rock, my sounding board, and the steady heartbeat beneath every chapter. Thank you for believing in me long before I believed in myself.

To my in-laws, Karen and Erik, thank you for welcoming me as your own and cheering me on, in my author journey and in life.

To my brother, Aiden—my best friend in every lifetime. Your support means more than you'll ever know.

To my incredible proofreaders, Paige, Abby, and Sheridan—thank you for combing through every line with care, precision, and patience.

To my beta readers, friend-supporters, and ARC team—D, Connor, Nicole, John, Keisha, Jessie, Esme, Courtney, Casey, Becky, Kay, Kinsey, Dela, Diana, Elle, Hannah, Heather, Kayla, Leah, Sage, Sue, Ag, Andrea, Vicky, and Mandy.

If I missed anyone, please know it wasn't from lack of gratitude but from the sheer astronomical number of people who touched this book at every stage. Your feedback, hype, honesty, and kindness shaped this story more than you realize.

And a huge thank-you to Christy Eckels—my biggest cheerleader throughout the editorial process. Thank you for being the teammate I didn't know I needed in publishing and the friend I'm so grateful to have in life.

To everyone who supported me, messaged me, encouraged me, or simply said, "Keep going"—this book carries pieces of all of you. Thank you for helping me bring it to life.

# About the Author

A. M. Walker is a debut novelist whose interest in psychological suspense emerged from a fascination with the ordinary facades that conceal extraordinary secrets. Walker holds a Master's degree in Communication a Bachelor's degree in Psychology, bringing both academic rigor and psychological insight to the methodical attention that drives domestic thriller narratives.

As a author and entrepreneur, Walker's work explores the intersection of suburban normalcy and hidden darkness, examining how apparently stable communities can harbor individuals whose internal lives are far more complex and dangerous than their external presentations would suggest. The author is particularly drawn to stories that examine the gradual erosion of moral boundaries and the ways that justified resentments can transform into something much more sinister.

When not writing, Walker enjoys gardening (strictly ornamental varieties), cooking, and long walks through neighborhoods where every house looks perfectly normal from the outside. She currently lives with a spouse who is very much alive and well and is in the early stages of family planning, during which she has vowed never to apply Ms. Volkova's teachings within her own home. She is also a devoted pet parent to three cats and a dog, residing in a location that will remain undisclosed for obvious reasons.

*Rooted in Silence* is Walker's debut novel. The sequel, *Bound in Botany*, is scheduled for release in March 2026.

# About Harbor & Stone Press

Harbor & Stone Press is an independent publishing house founded to give writers a clear, supportive path to publication without the long wait times or gatekeeping of traditional publishing.

We partner with authors to provide professional editing, design, and marketing services, all while keeping the process transparent, flexible, and author-focused.

Our mission is simple: to help great stories find their way into the world. Whether you're publishing your first book or building a series, Harbor & Stone Press is committed to quality, creativity, and collaboration every step of the way.

For more about us, visit: harborandstonepress.com

www.ingramcontent.com/pod-product-compliance
Lightning Source LLC
Chambersburg PA
CBHW050032120726
47903CB00006B/2005